My Little Pony
Spirit of the Forest

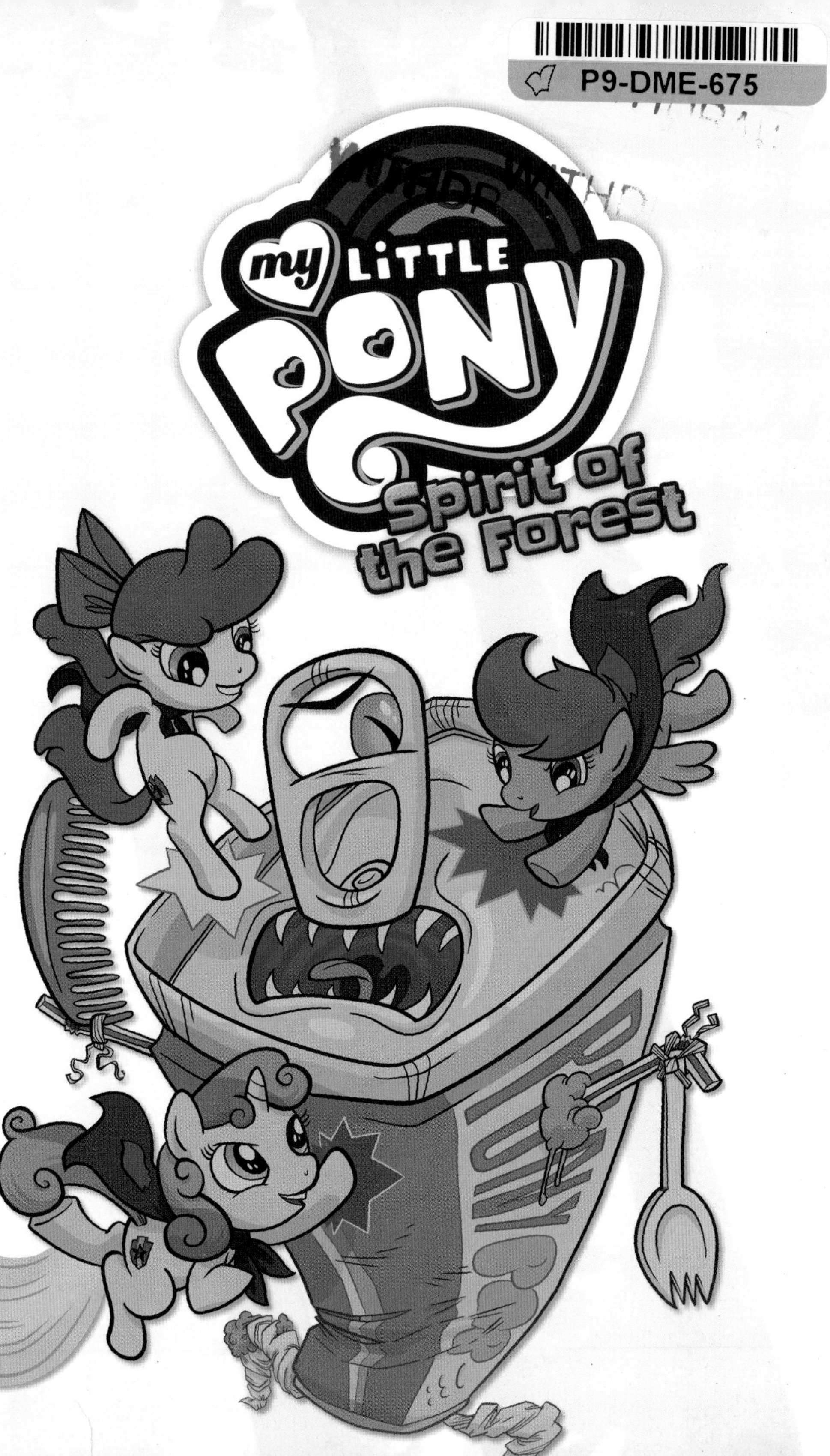

IDW

Licensed By: Hasbro

Special thanks to Tayla Reo , Ed Lane, Beth Artale, and Michael Kelly.

ISBN: 978-1-68405-609-5 22 21 20 19 1 2 3 4

Chris Ryall, President, Publisher, & CCO
John Barber, Editor-In-Chief
Cara Morrison, Chief Financial Officer
Matt Ruzicka, Chief Accounting Officer
David Hedgecock, Associate Publisher
Jerry Bennington, VP of New Product Development
Lorelei Bunjes, VP of Digital Services
Justin Eisinger, Editorial Director, Graphic Novels & Collections
Eric Moss, Senior Director, Licensing and Business Development

Ted Adams and Robbie Robbins, IDW Founders

For international rights, please contact
licensing@idwpublishing.com

Originally published as MY LITTLE PONY: SPIRIT OF THE FOREST issues #1–3.

COVER ARTIST
Brenda Hickey

COLLECTION EDITORS
Justin Eisinger
AND **Alonzo Simon**

COLLECTION DESIGNER
Claudia Chong

my LiTTLE PONY

Spirit of the Forest

WRITTEN BY
Ted Anderson

ART BY
Brenda Hickey

COLORS BY
Heather Breckel

LETTERS BY
Neil Uyetake AND **Christa Miesner**

SERIES EDITOR
Megan Brown

SERIES GROUP EDITOR
Bobby Curnow

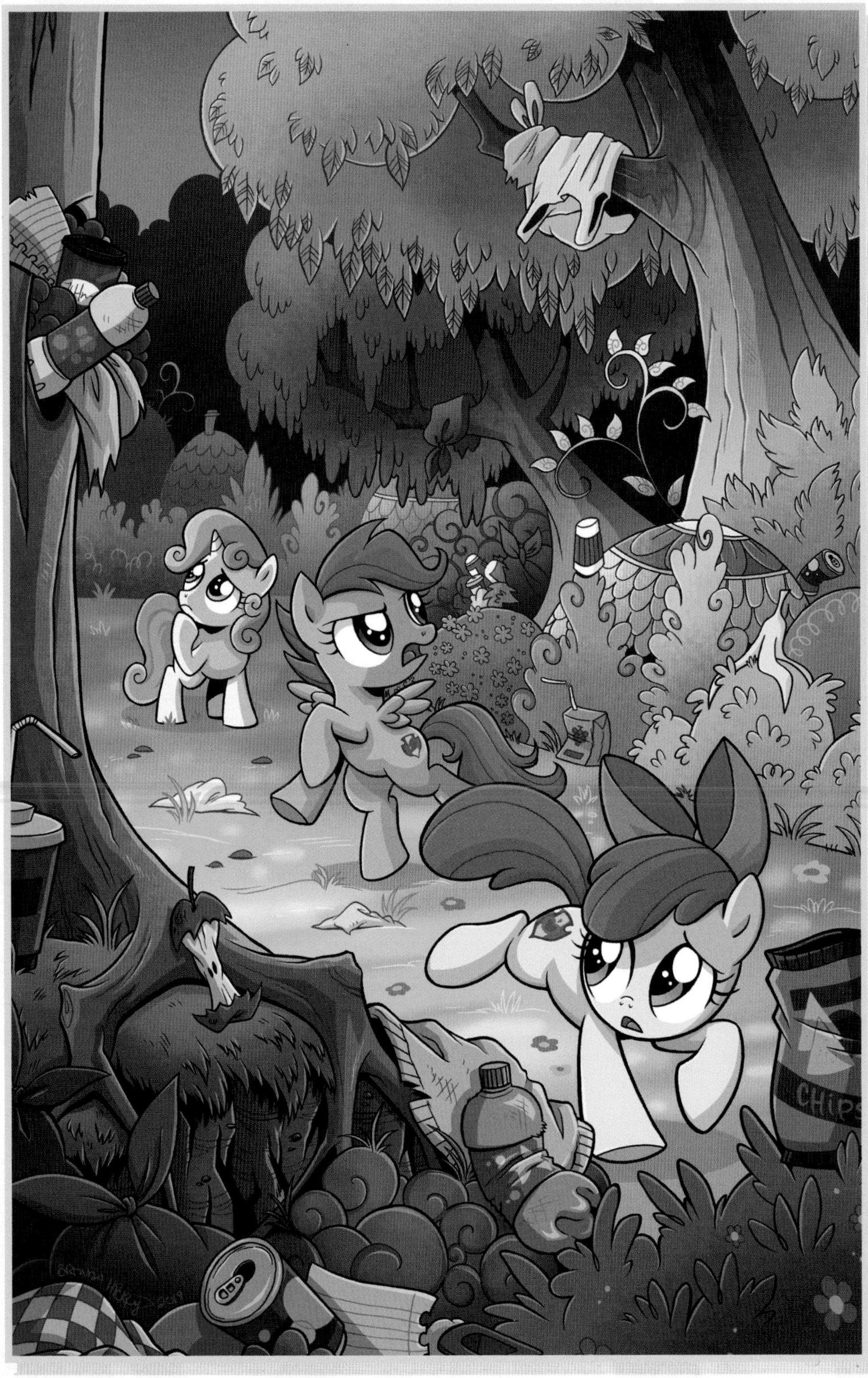

ART BY **Brenda Hickey**

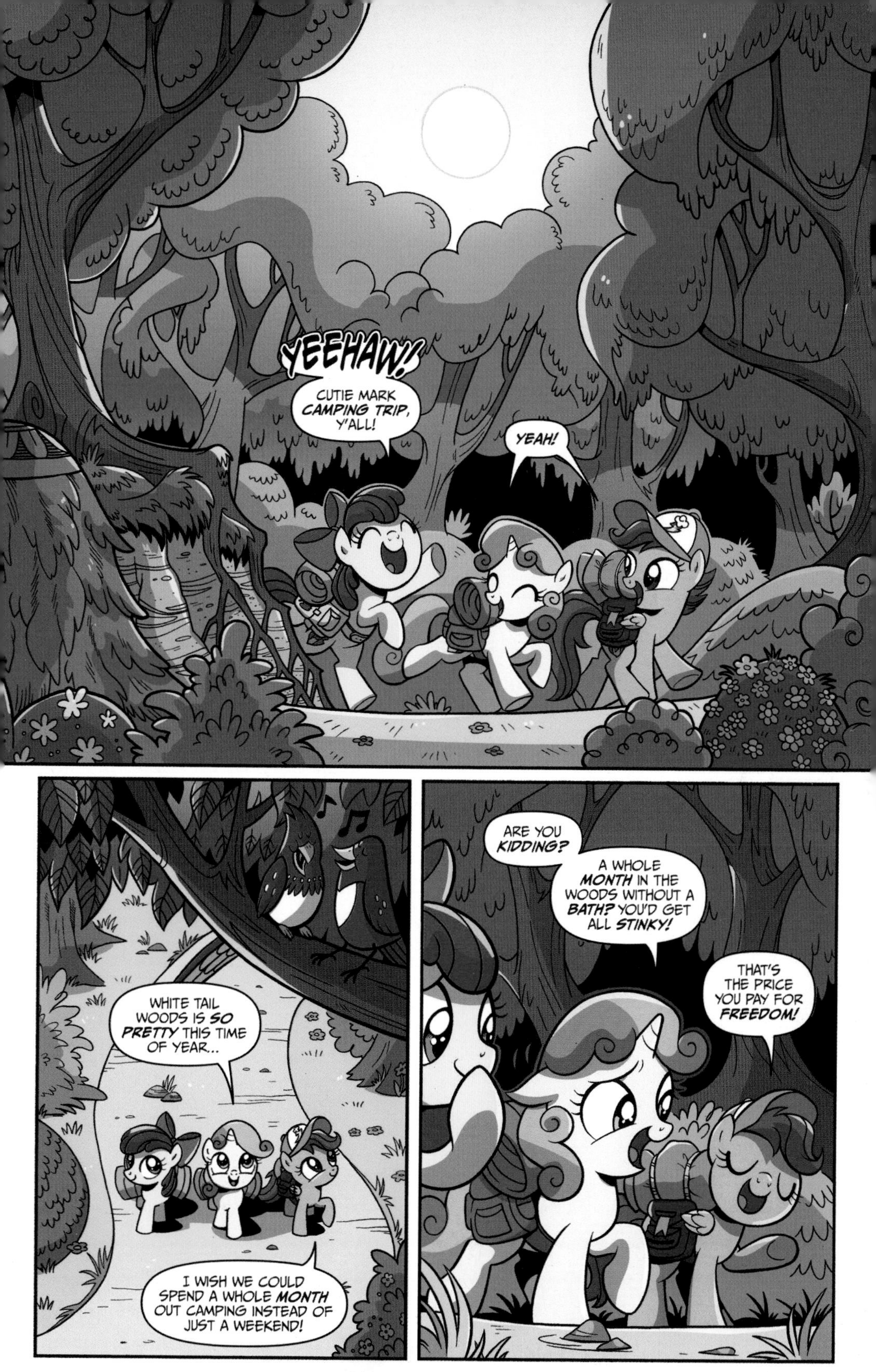
YEEHAW!
CUTIE MARK CAMPING TRIP, Y'ALL!
YEAH!
WHITE TAIL WOODS IS SO PRETTY THIS TIME OF YEAR...
I WISH WE COULD SPEND A WHOLE MONTH OUT CAMPING INSTEAD OF JUST A WEEKEND!
ARE YOU KIDDING?
A WHOLE MONTH IN THE WOODS WITHOUT A BATH? YOU'D GET ALL STINKY!
THAT'S THE PRICE YOU PAY FOR FREEDOM!

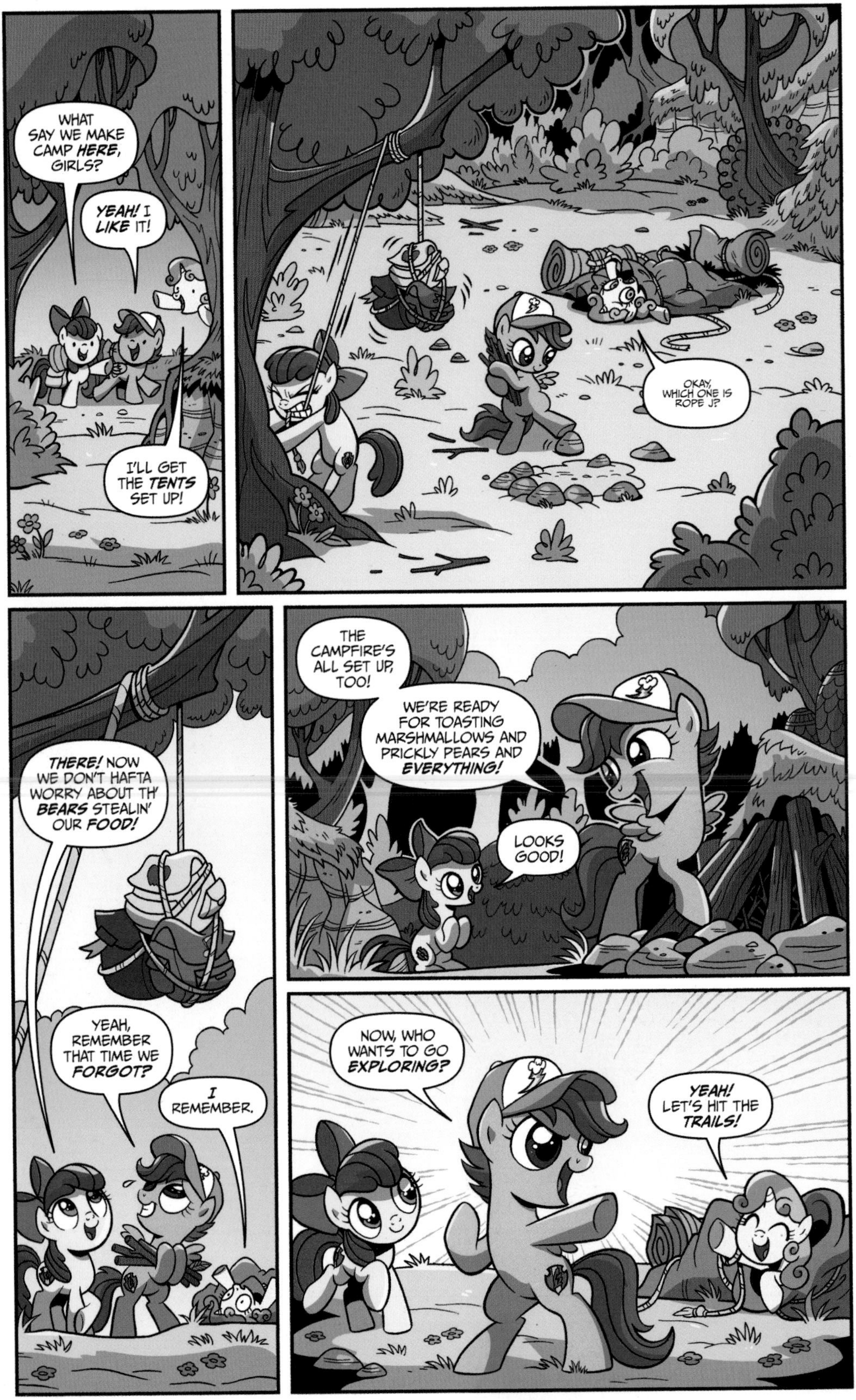
WHAT SAY WE MAKE CAMP *HERE*, GIRLS?
YEAH! I *LIKE* IT!
I'LL GET THE *TENTS* SET UP!
OKAY, WHICH ONE IS ROPE J?
THERE! NOW WE DON'T HAFTA WORRY ABOUT TH' *BEARS* STEALIN' OUR *FOOD!*
YEAH, REMEMBER THAT TIME WE *FORGOT?*
I REMEMBER.
THE CAMPFIRE'S ALL SET UP, TOO!
WE'RE READY FOR TOASTING MARSHMALLOWS AND PRICKLY PEARS AND *EVERYTHING!*
LOOKS GOOD!
NOW, WHO WANTS TO GO *EXPLORING?*
YEAH! LET'S HIT THE *TRAILS!*

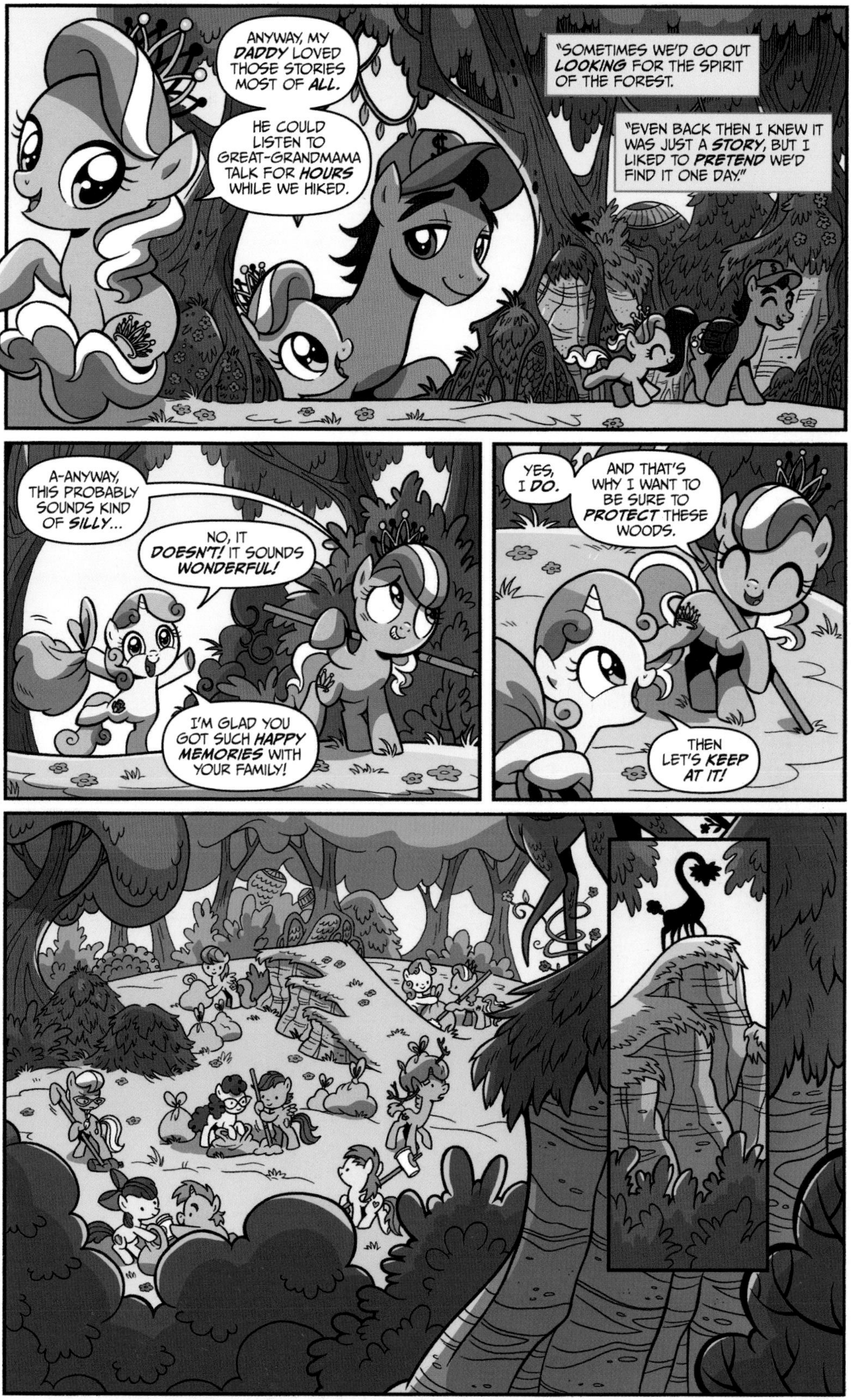

ANYWAY, MY DADDY LOVED THOSE STORIES MOST OF ALL.
HE COULD LISTEN TO GREAT-GRANDMAMA TALK FOR HOURS WHILE WE HIKED.
"SOMETIMES WE'D GO OUT LOOKING FOR THE SPIRIT OF THE FOREST.
"EVEN BACK THEN I KNEW IT WAS JUST A STORY, BUT I LIKED TO PRETEND WE'D FIND IT ONE DAY."
A-ANYWAY, THIS PROBABLY SOUNDS KIND OF SILLY...
NO, IT DOESN'T! IT SOUNDS WONDERFUL!
I'M GLAD YOU GOT SUCH HAPPY MEMORIES WITH YOUR FAMILY!
YES, I DO.
AND THAT'S WHY I WANT TO BE SURE TO PROTECT THESE WOODS.
THEN LET'S KEEP AT IT!

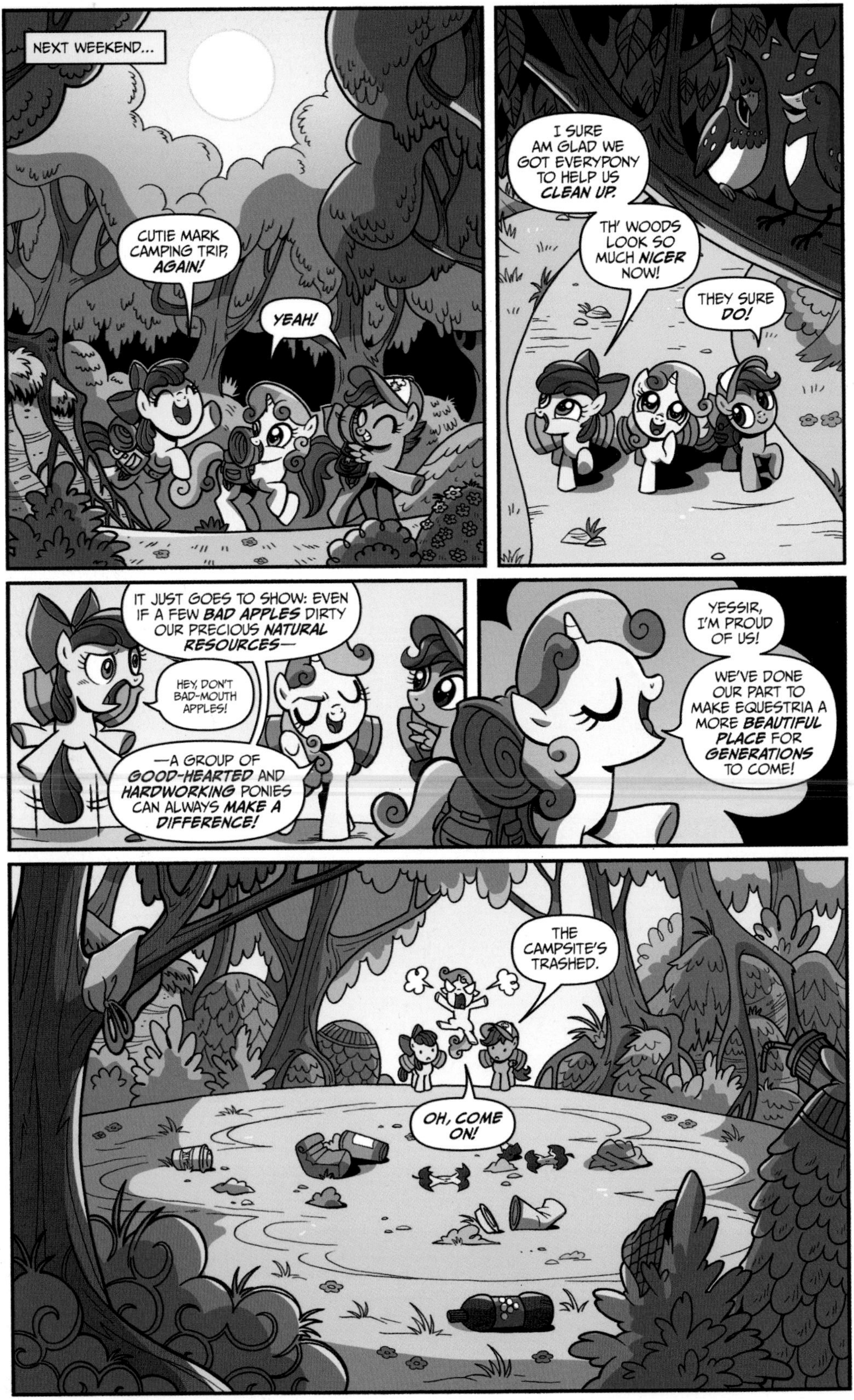
NEXT WEEKEND...
CUTIE MARK CAMPING TRIP, AGAIN!
YEAH!
I SURE AM GLAD WE GOT EVERYPONY TO HELP US CLEAN UP.
TH' WOODS LOOK SO MUCH NICER NOW!
THEY SURE DO!
IT JUST GOES TO SHOW: EVEN IF A FEW BAD APPLES DIRTY OUR PRECIOUS NATURAL RESOURCES—
HEY, DON'T BAD-MOUTH APPLES!
—A GROUP OF GOOD-HEARTED AND HARDWORKING PONIES CAN ALWAYS MAKE A DIFFERENCE!
YESSIR, I'M PROUD OF US!
WE'VE DONE OUR PART TO MAKE EQUESTRIA A MORE BEAUTIFUL PLACE FOR GENERATIONS TO COME!
THE CAMPSITE'S TRASHED.
OH, COME ON!

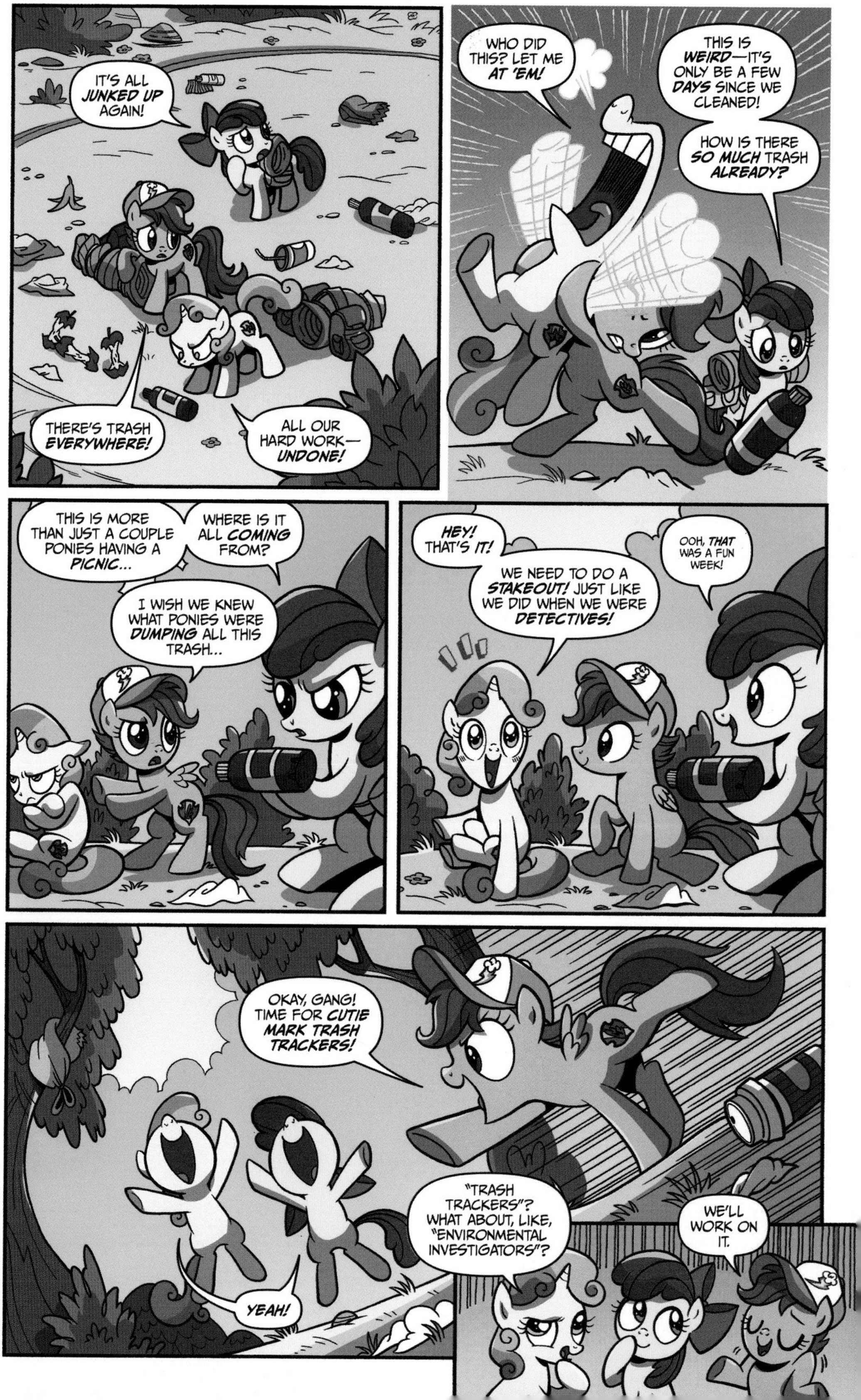

IT'S ALL JUNKED UP AGAIN!
THERE'S TRASH EVERYWHERE!
ALL OUR HARD WORK— UNDONE!
WHO DID THIS? LET ME AT 'EM!
THIS IS WEIRD—IT'S ONLY BE A FEW DAYS SINCE WE CLEANED!
HOW IS THERE SO MUCH TRASH ALREADY?
THIS IS MORE THAN JUST A COUPLE PONIES HAVING A PICNIC...
WHERE IS IT ALL COMING FROM?
I WISH WE KNEW WHAT PONIES WERE DUMPING ALL THIS TRASH...
HEY! THAT'S IT!
OOH, THAT WAS A FUN WEEK!
WE NEED TO DO A STAKEOUT! JUST LIKE WE DID WHEN WE WERE DETECTIVES!
OKAY, GANG! TIME FOR CUTIE MARK TRASH TRACKERS!
YEAH!
"TRASH TRACKERS"? WHAT ABOUT, LIKE, "ENVIRONMENTAL INVESTIGATORS"?
WE'LL WORK ON IT.

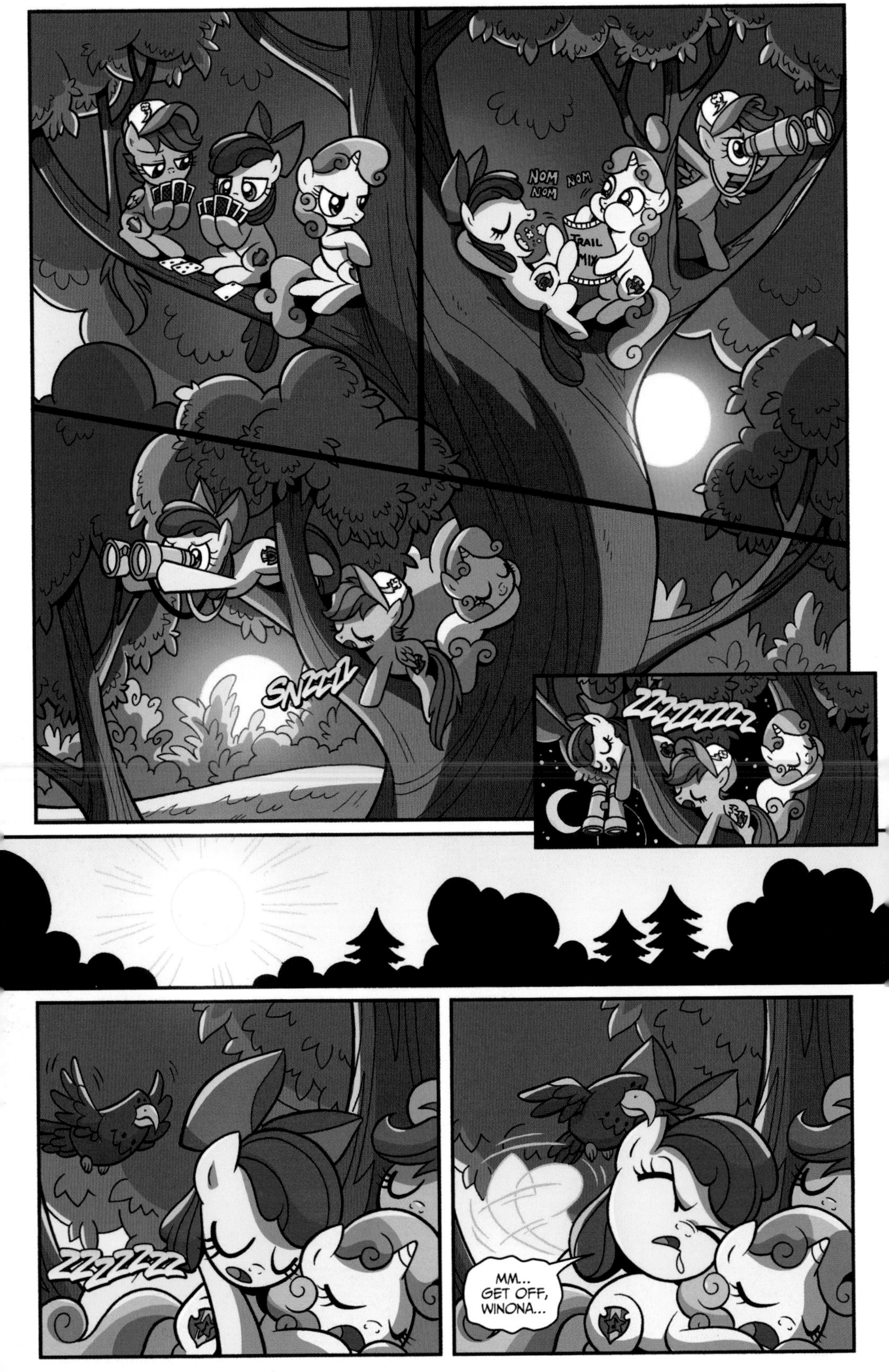
NOM NOM NOM NOM
TRAIL MIX
SNZZZ
ZZZZZZZZZ
ZZZZZZ
MM... GET OFF, WINONA...

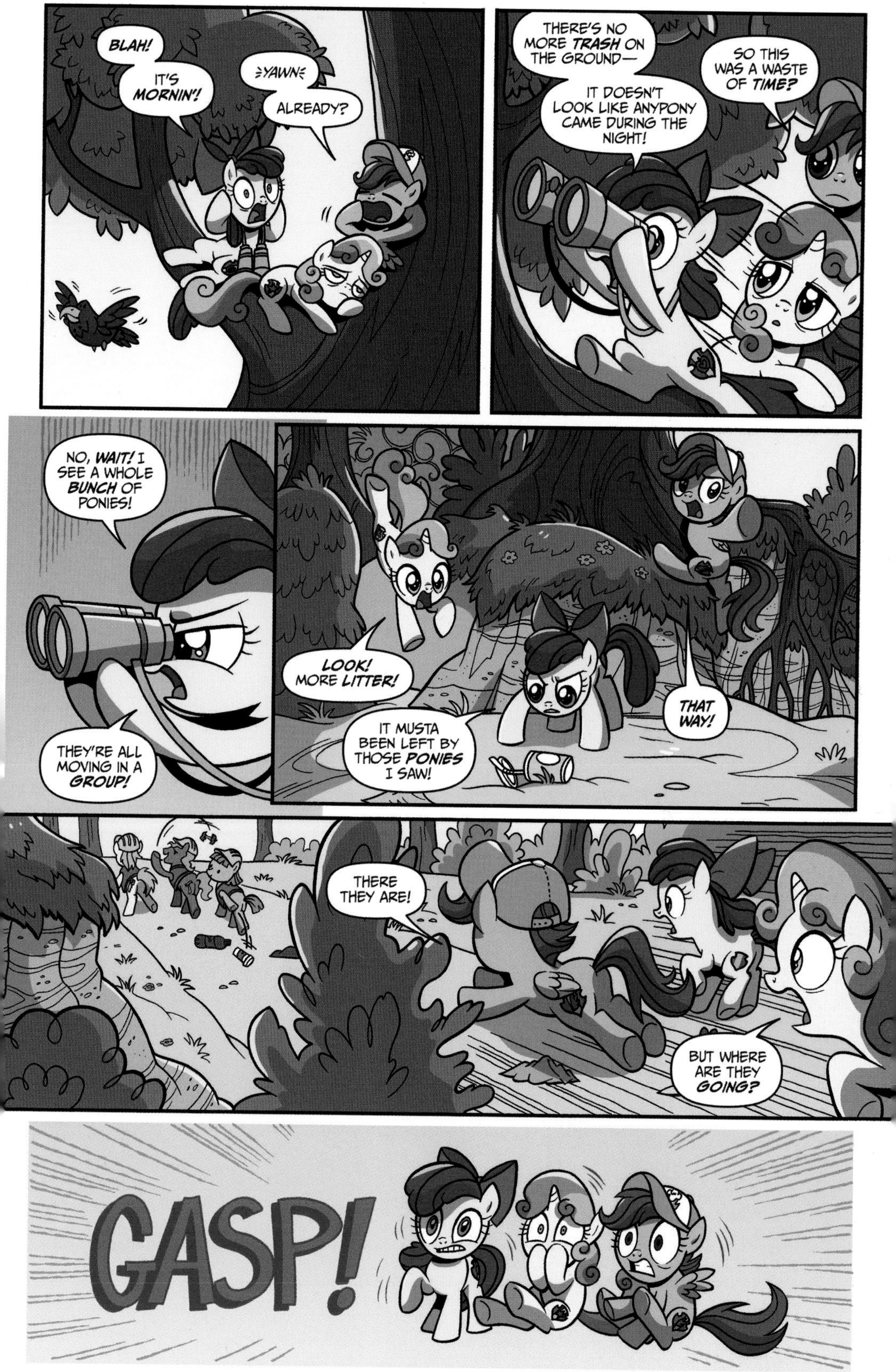
BLAH!
IT'S MORNIN'!
≶YAWN≶
ALREADY?
THERE'S NO MORE TRASH ON THE GROUND—
IT DOESN'T LOOK LIKE ANYPONY CAME DURING THE NIGHT!
SO THIS WAS A WASTE OF TIME?
NO, WAIT! I SEE A WHOLE BUNCH OF PONIES!
THEY'RE ALL MOVING IN A GROUP!
LOOK! MORE LITTER!
IT MUSTA BEEN LEFT BY THOSE PONIES I SAW!
THAT WAY!
THERE THEY ARE!
BUT WHERE ARE THEY GOING?
GASP!

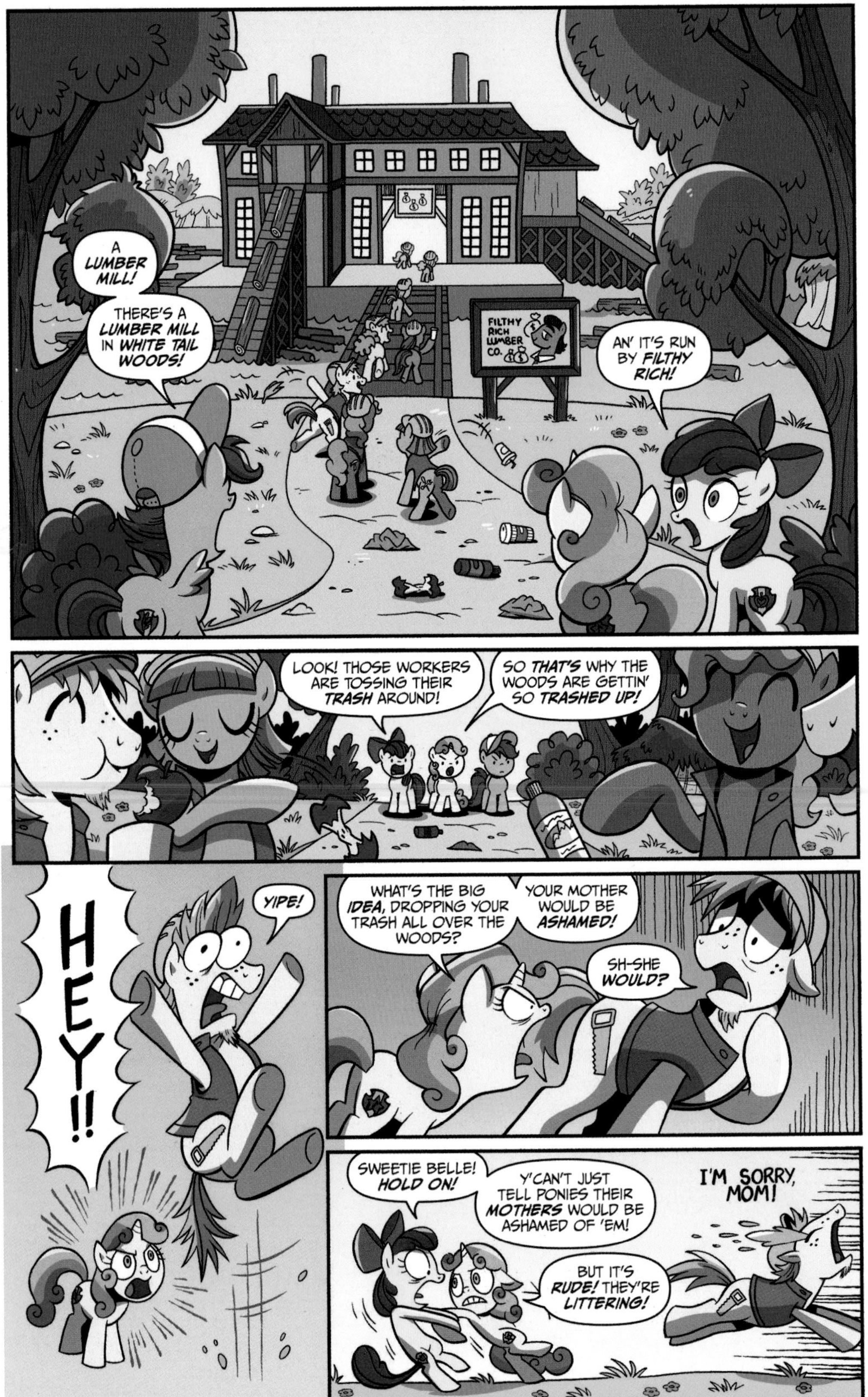
A LUMBER MILL!
THERE'S A LUMBER MILL IN WHITE TAIL WOODS!
FILTHY RICH LUMBER CO.
AN' IT'S RUN BY FILTHY RICH!
LOOK! THOSE WORKERS ARE TOSSING THEIR TRASH AROUND!
SO THAT'S WHY THE WOODS ARE GETTIN' SO TRASHED UP!
HEY!!
YIPE!
WHAT'S THE BIG IDEA, DROPPING YOUR TRASH ALL OVER THE WOODS?
YOUR MOTHER WOULD BE ASHAMED!
SH-SHE WOULD?
SWEETIE BELLE! HOLD ON!
Y'CAN'T JUST TELL PONIES THEIR MOTHERS WOULD BE ASHAMED OF 'EM!
I'M SORRY, MOM!
BUT IT'S RUDE! THEY'RE LITTERING!

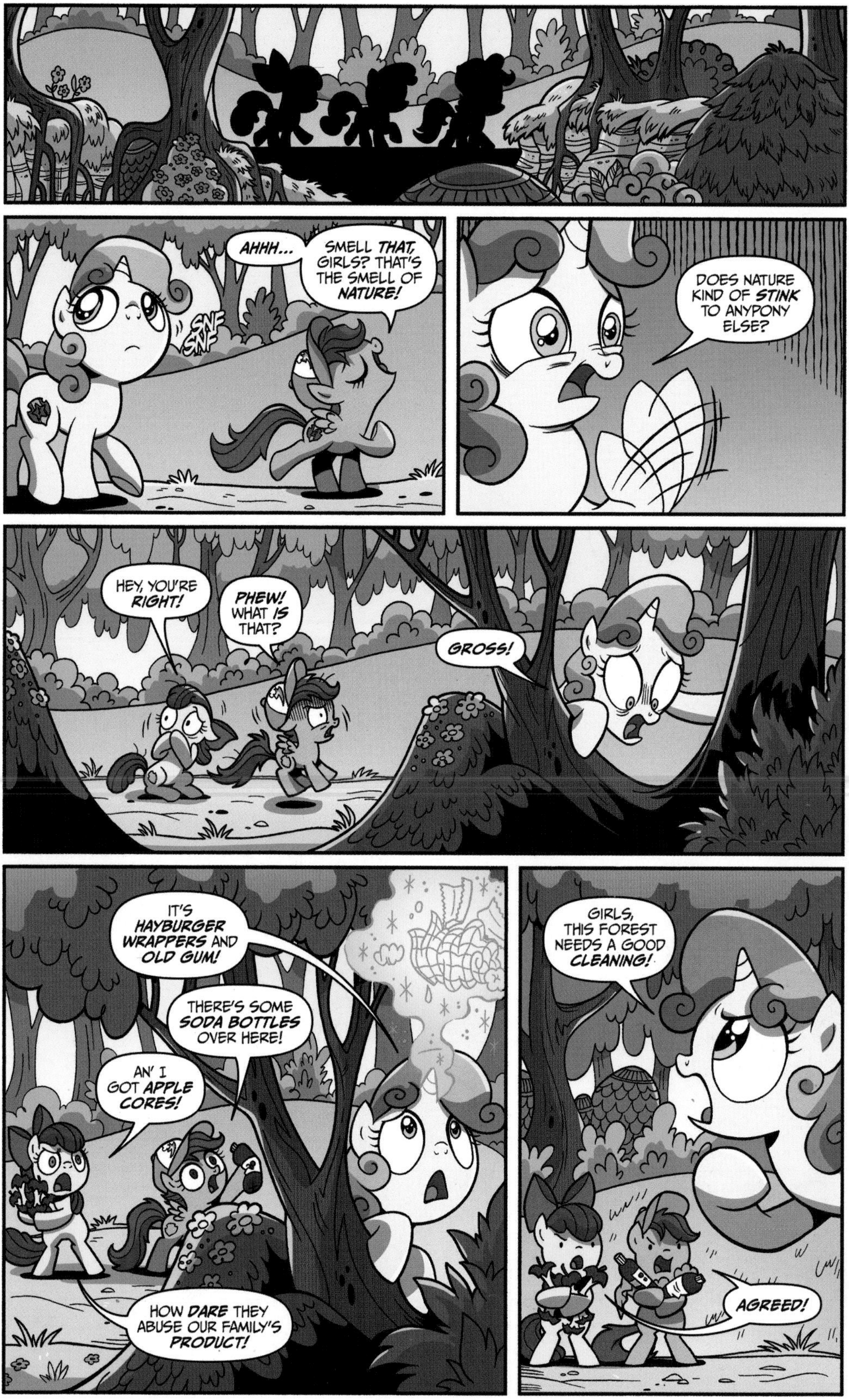
AHHH...
SMELL THAT, GIRLS? THAT'S THE SMELL OF NATURE!
SNF SNF
DOES NATURE KIND OF STINK TO ANYPONY ELSE?
HEY, YOU'RE RIGHT!
PHEW! WHAT IS THAT?
GROSS!
IT'S HAYBURGER WRAPPERS AND OLD GUM!
THERE'S SOME SODA BOTTLES OVER HERE!
AN' I GOT APPLE CORES!
HOW DARE THEY ABUSE OUR FAMILY'S PRODUCT!
GIRLS, THIS FOREST NEEDS A GOOD CLEANING!
AGREED!

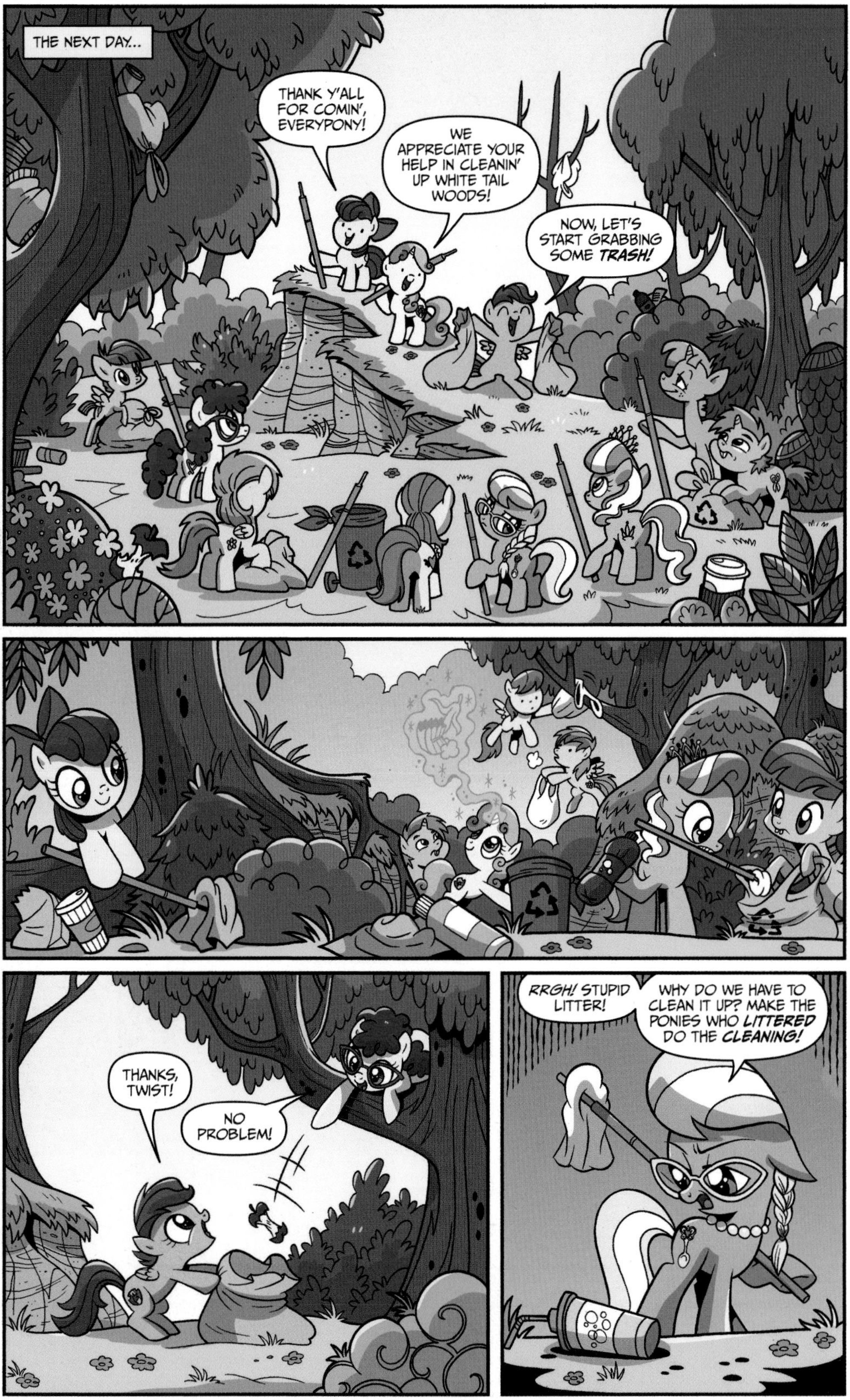
THE NEXT DAY...
THANK Y'ALL FOR COMIN', EVERYPONY!
WE APPRECIATE YOUR HELP IN CLEANIN' UP WHITE TAIL WOODS!
NOW, LET'S START GRABBING SOME *TRASH!*
THANKS, TWIST!
NO PROBLEM!
RRGH! STUPID LITTER!
WHY DO WE HAVE TO CLEAN IT UP? MAKE THE PONIES WHO *LITTERED* DO THE *CLEANING!*

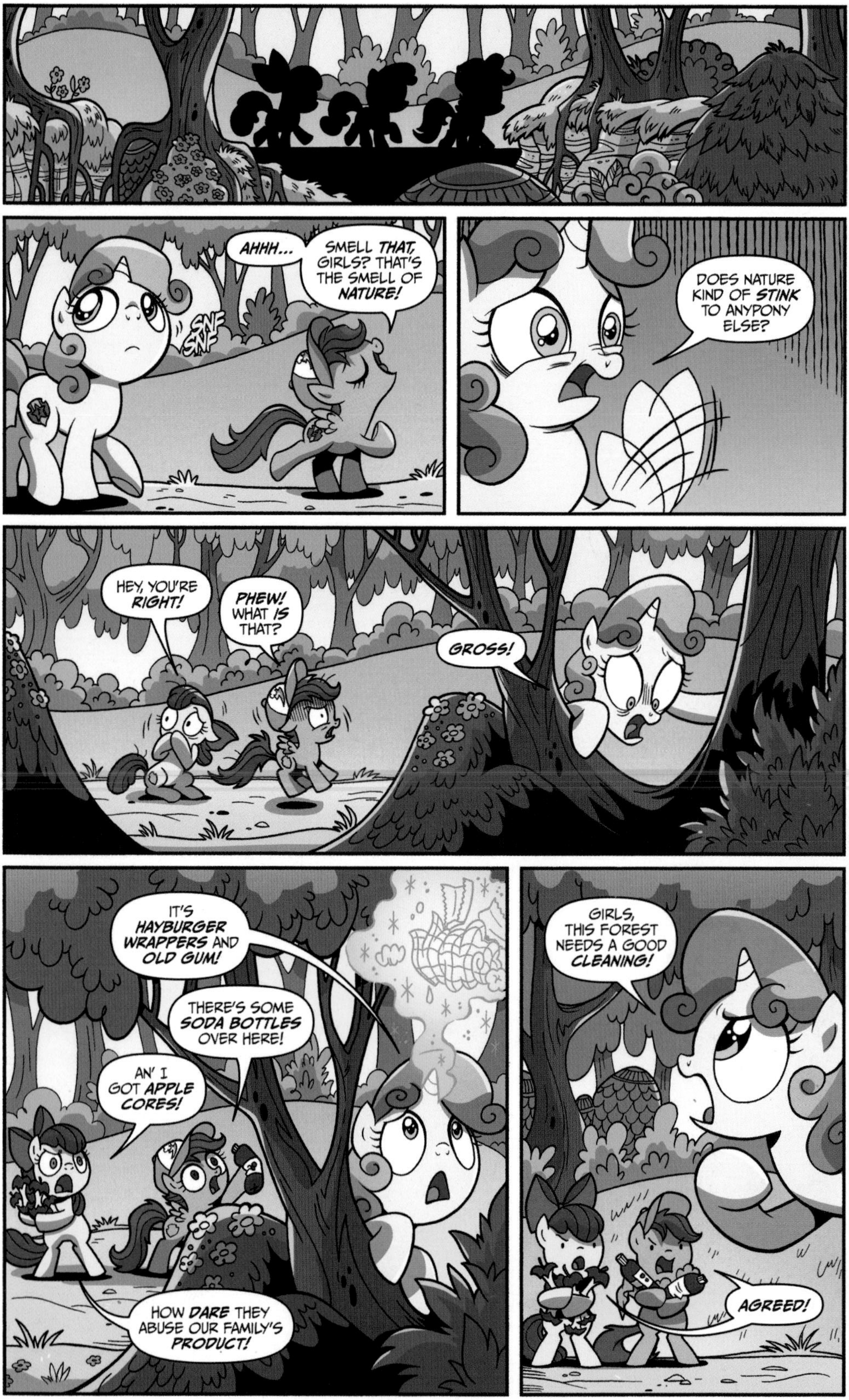
AHHH...
SMELL THAT, GIRLS? THAT'S THE SMELL OF NATURE!
SNF SNF
DOES NATURE KIND OF STINK TO ANYPONY ELSE?
HEY, YOU'RE RIGHT!
PHEW! WHAT IS THAT?
GROSS!
IT'S HAYBURGER WRAPPERS AND OLD GUM!
THERE'S SOME SODA BOTTLES OVER HERE!
AN' I GOT APPLE CORES!
HOW DARE THEY ABUSE OUR FAMILY'S PRODUCT!
GIRLS, THIS FOREST NEEDS A GOOD CLEANING!
AGREED!

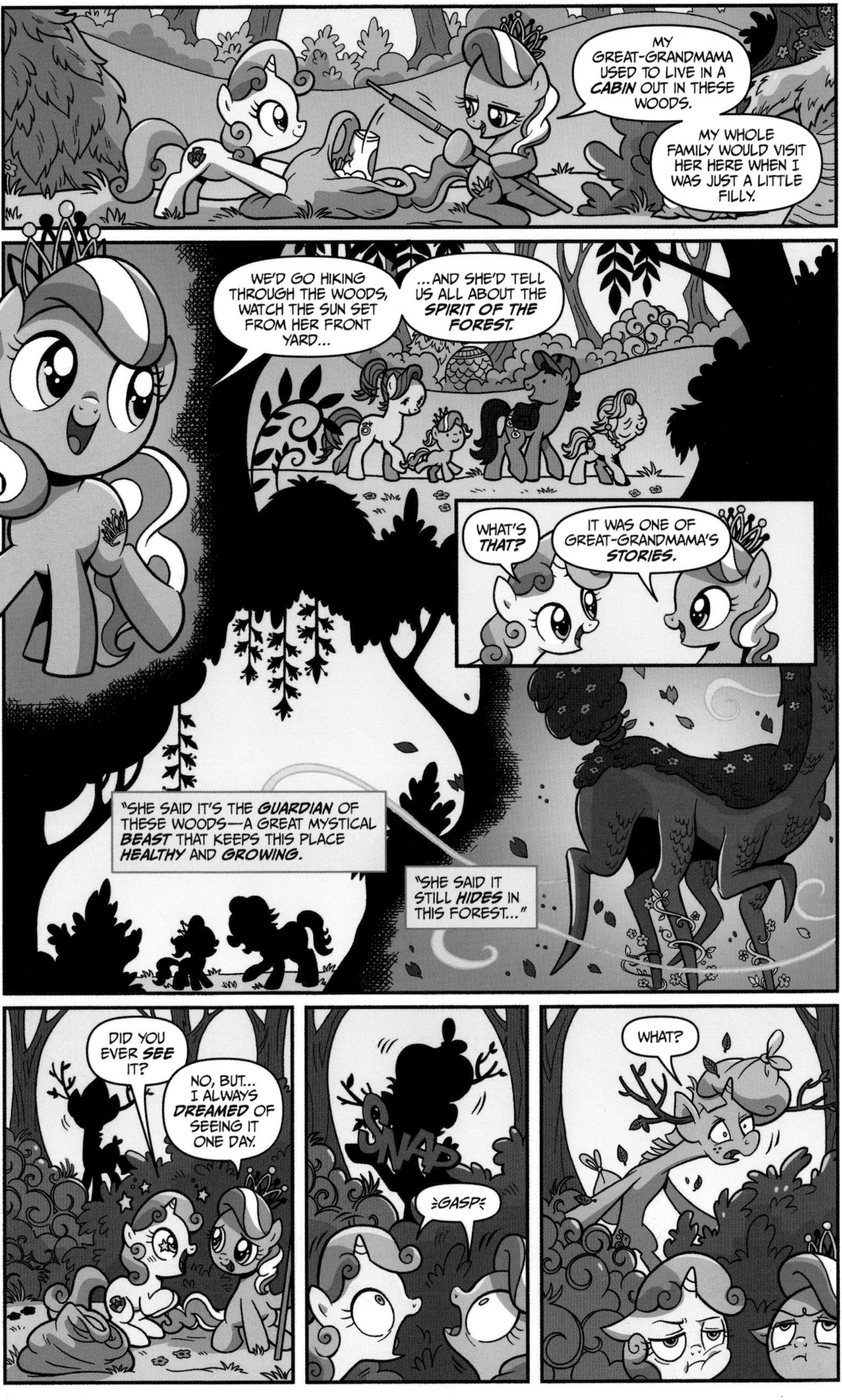
MY GREAT-GRANDMAMA USED TO LIVE IN A CABIN OUT IN THESE WOODS.
MY WHOLE FAMILY WOULD VISIT HER HERE WHEN I WAS JUST A LITTLE FILLY.
WE'D GO HIKING THROUGH THE WOODS, WATCH THE SUN SET FROM HER FRONT YARD...
...AND SHE'D TELL US ALL ABOUT THE SPIRIT OF THE FOREST.
WHAT'S THAT?
IT WAS ONE OF GREAT-GRANDMAMA'S STORIES.
"SHE SAID IT'S THE GUARDIAN OF THESE WOODS—A GREAT MYSTICAL BEAST THAT KEEPS THIS PLACE HEALTHY AND GROWING.
"SHE SAID IT STILL HIDES IN THIS FOREST..."
DID YOU EVER SEE IT?
NO, BUT... I ALWAYS DREAMED OF SEEING IT ONE DAY.
SNAP
GASP
WHAT?

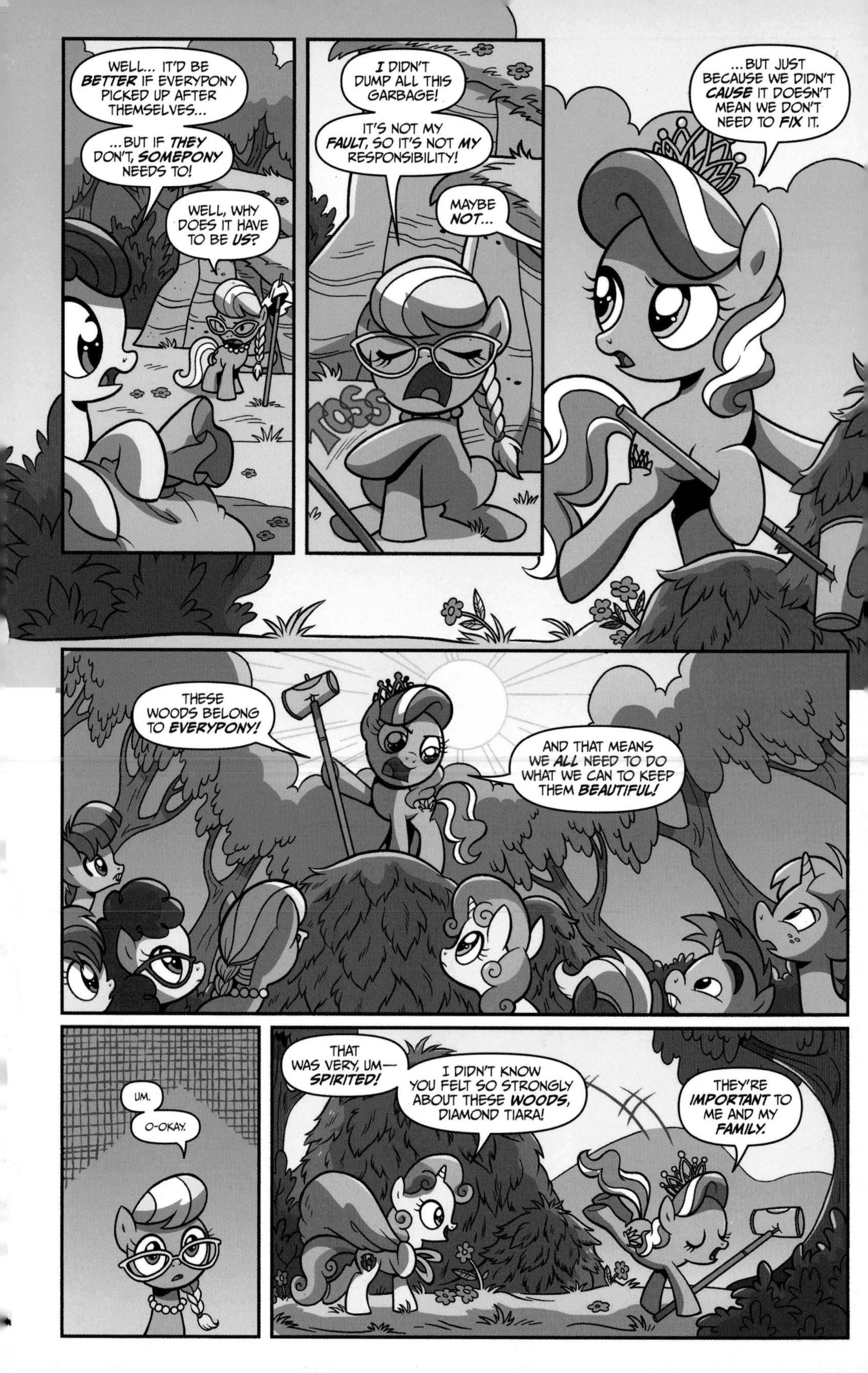
WELL... IT'D BE BETTER IF EVERYPONY PICKED UP AFTER THEMSELVES...
...BUT IF THEY DON'T, SOMEPONY NEEDS TO!
WELL, WHY DOES IT HAVE TO BE US?
I DIDN'T DUMP ALL THIS GARBAGE!
IT'S NOT MY FAULT, SO IT'S NOT MY RESPONSIBILITY!
TOSS
MAYBE NOT...
...BUT JUST BECAUSE WE DIDN'T CAUSE IT DOESN'T MEAN WE DON'T NEED TO FIX IT.
THESE WOODS BELONG TO EVERYPONY!
AND THAT MEANS WE ALL NEED TO DO WHAT WE CAN TO KEEP THEM BEAUTIFUL!
UM.
O-OKAY.
THAT WAS VERY, UM— SPIRITED!
I DIDN'T KNOW YOU FELT SO STRONGLY ABOUT THESE WOODS, DIAMOND TIARA!
THEY'RE IMPORTANT TO ME AND MY FAMILY.

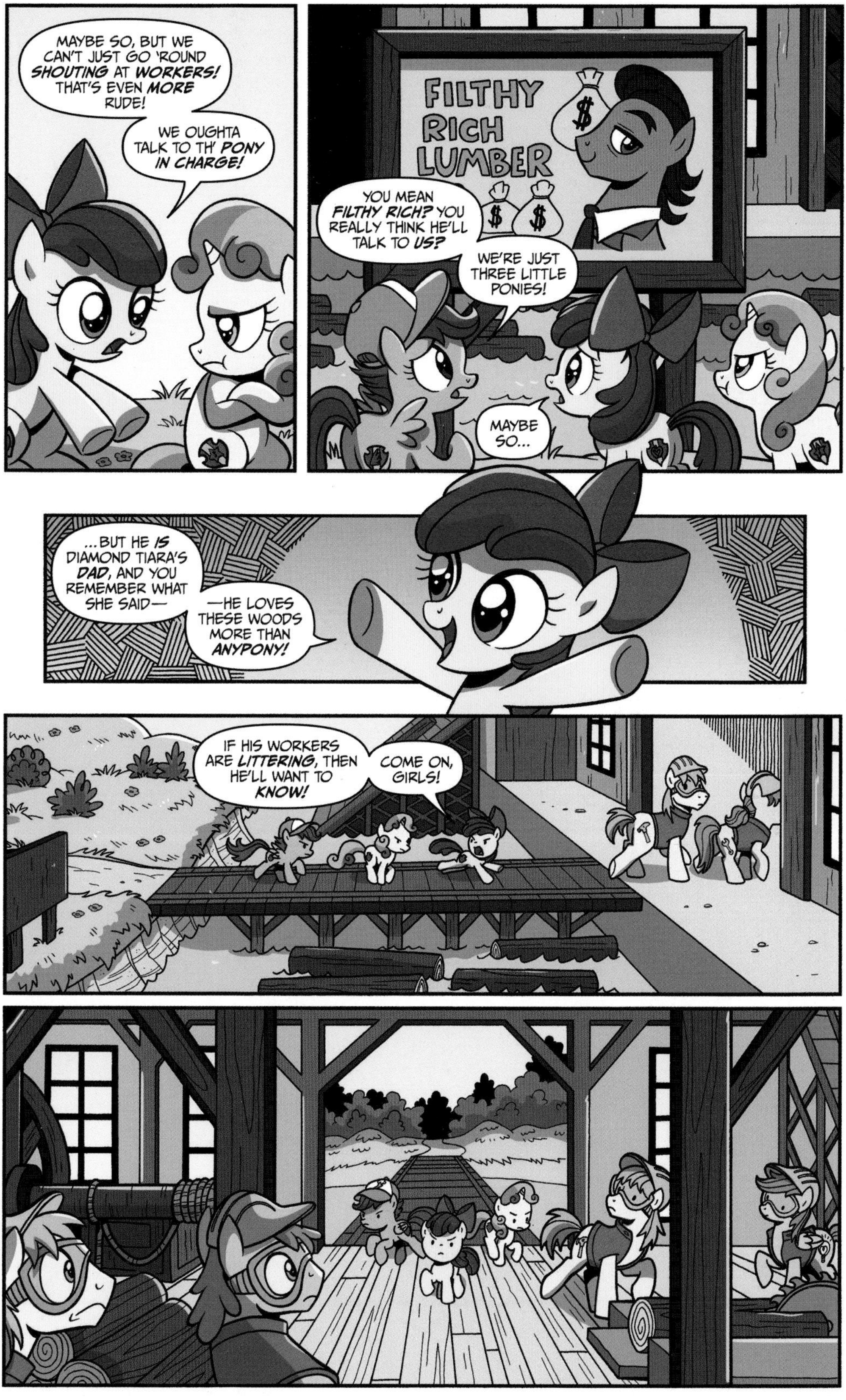
MAYBE SO, BUT WE CAN'T JUST GO 'ROUND SHOUTING AT WORKERS! THAT'S EVEN MORE RUDE!
WE OUGHTA TALK TO TH' PONY IN CHARGE!
FILTHY RICH LUMBER
YOU MEAN FILTHY RICH? YOU REALLY THINK HE'LL TALK TO US?
WE'RE JUST THREE LITTLE PONIES!
MAYBE SO...
...BUT HE IS DIAMOND TIARA'S DAD, AND YOU REMEMBER WHAT SHE SAID—
—HE LOVES THESE WOODS MORE THAN ANYPONY!
IF HIS WORKERS ARE LITTERING, THEN HE'LL WANT TO KNOW!
COME ON, GIRLS!

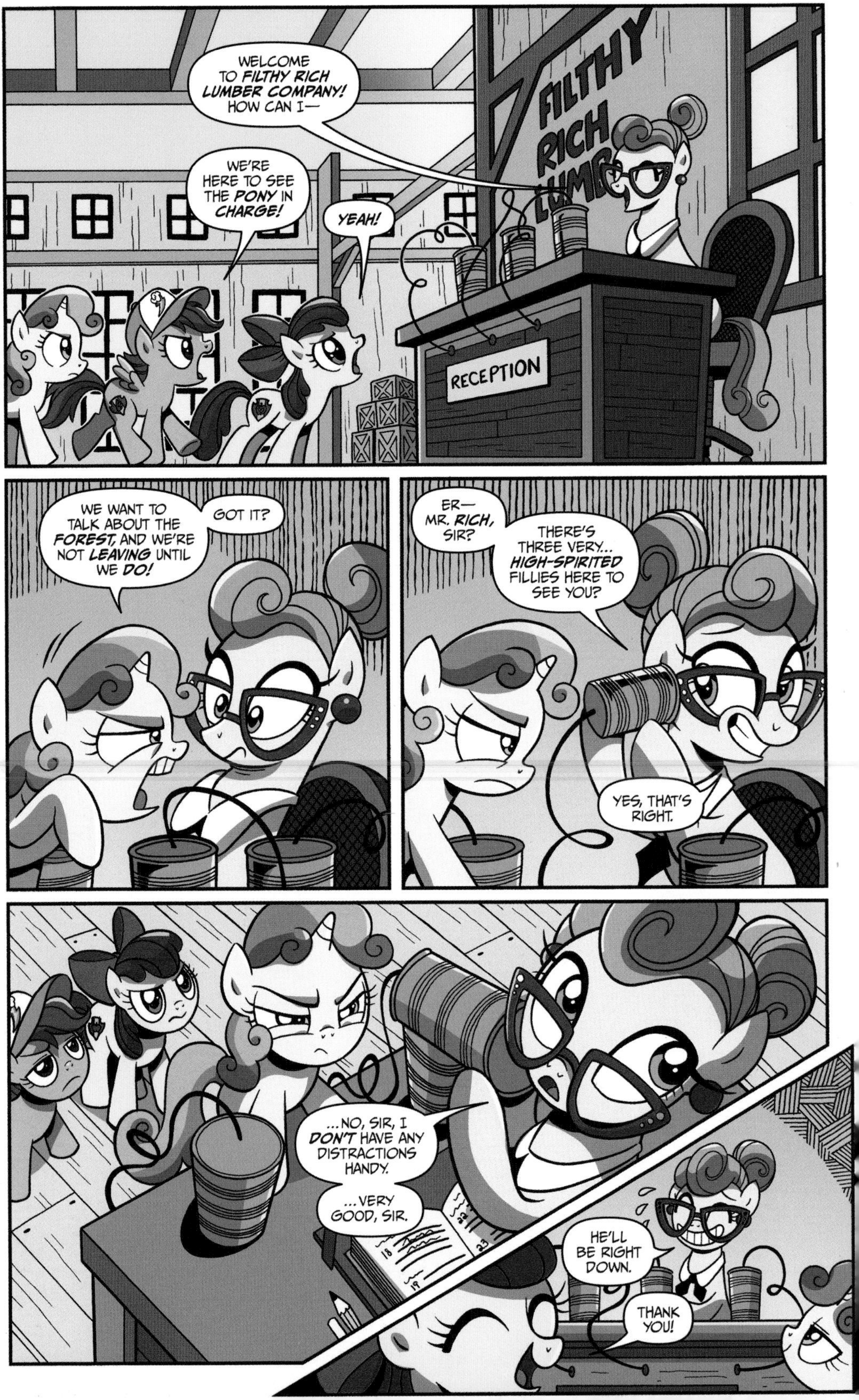
WELCOME TO FILTHY RICH LUMBER COMPANY! HOW CAN I—
FILTHY RICH LUMB
WE'RE HERE TO SEE THE PONY IN CHARGE!
YEAH!
RECEPTION
WE WANT TO TALK ABOUT THE FOREST, AND WE'RE NOT LEAVING UNTIL WE DO!
GOT IT?
ER— MR. RICH, SIR?
THERE'S THREE VERY... HIGH-SPIRITED FILLIES HERE TO SEE YOU?
YES, THAT'S RIGHT.
...NO, SIR, I DON'T HAVE ANY DISTRACTIONS HANDY.
...VERY GOOD, SIR.
HE'LL BE RIGHT DOWN.
THANK YOU!

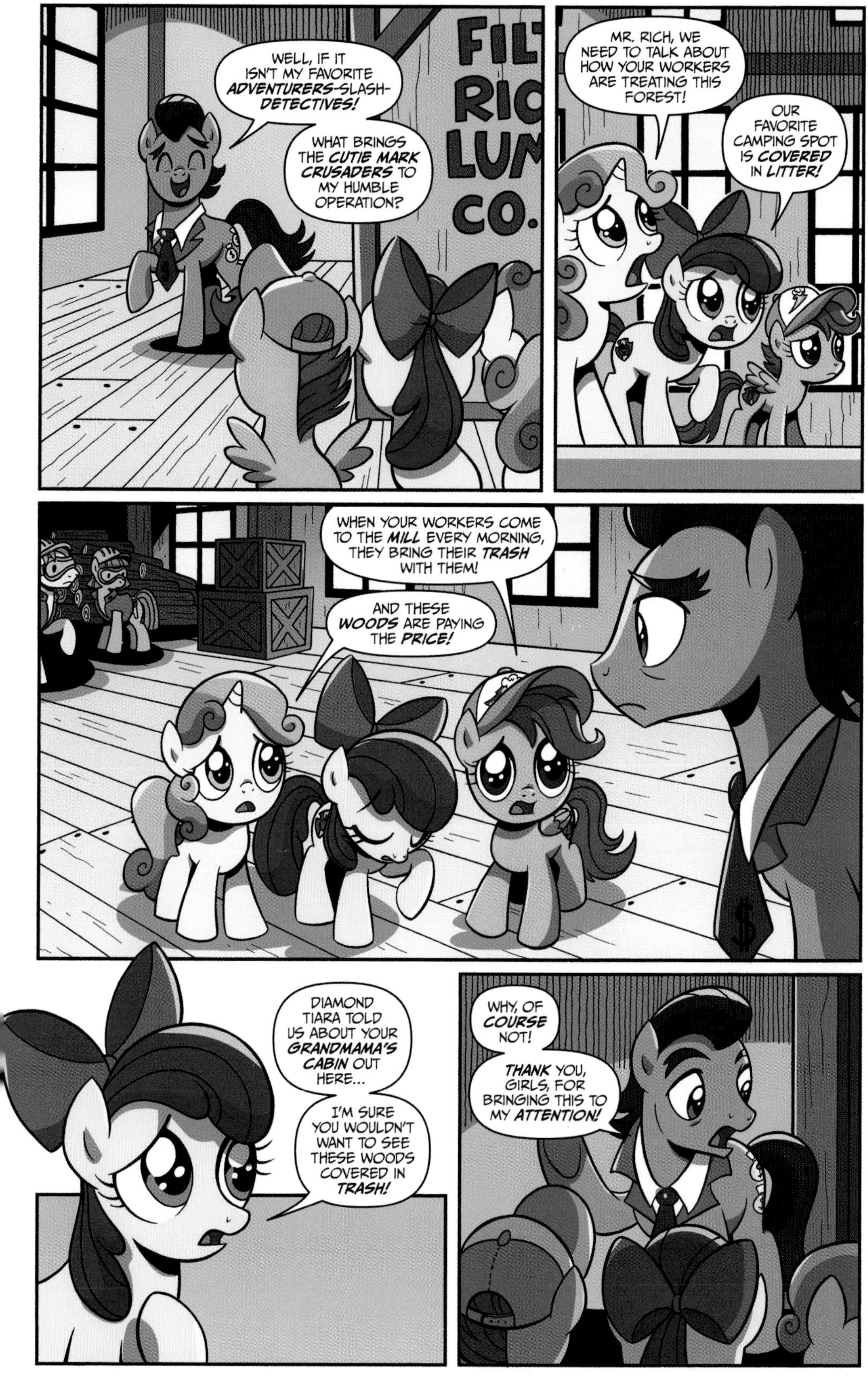
FILT RIC LUM CO.
WELL, IF IT ISN'T MY FAVORITE ADVENTURERS-SLASH-DETECTIVES!
WHAT BRINGS THE CUTIE MARK CRUSADERS TO MY HUMBLE OPERATION?
MR. RICH, WE NEED TO TALK ABOUT HOW YOUR WORKERS ARE TREATING THIS FOREST!
OUR FAVORITE CAMPING SPOT IS COVERED IN LITTER!
WHEN YOUR WORKERS COME TO THE MILL EVERY MORNING, THEY BRING THEIR TRASH WITH THEM!
AND THESE WOODS ARE PAYING THE PRICE!
DIAMOND TIARA TOLD US ABOUT YOUR GRANDMAMA'S CABIN OUT HERE...
I'M SURE YOU WOULDN'T WANT TO SEE THESE WOODS COVERED IN TRASH!
WHY, OF COURSE NOT!
THANK YOU, GIRLS, FOR BRINGING THIS TO MY ATTENTION!

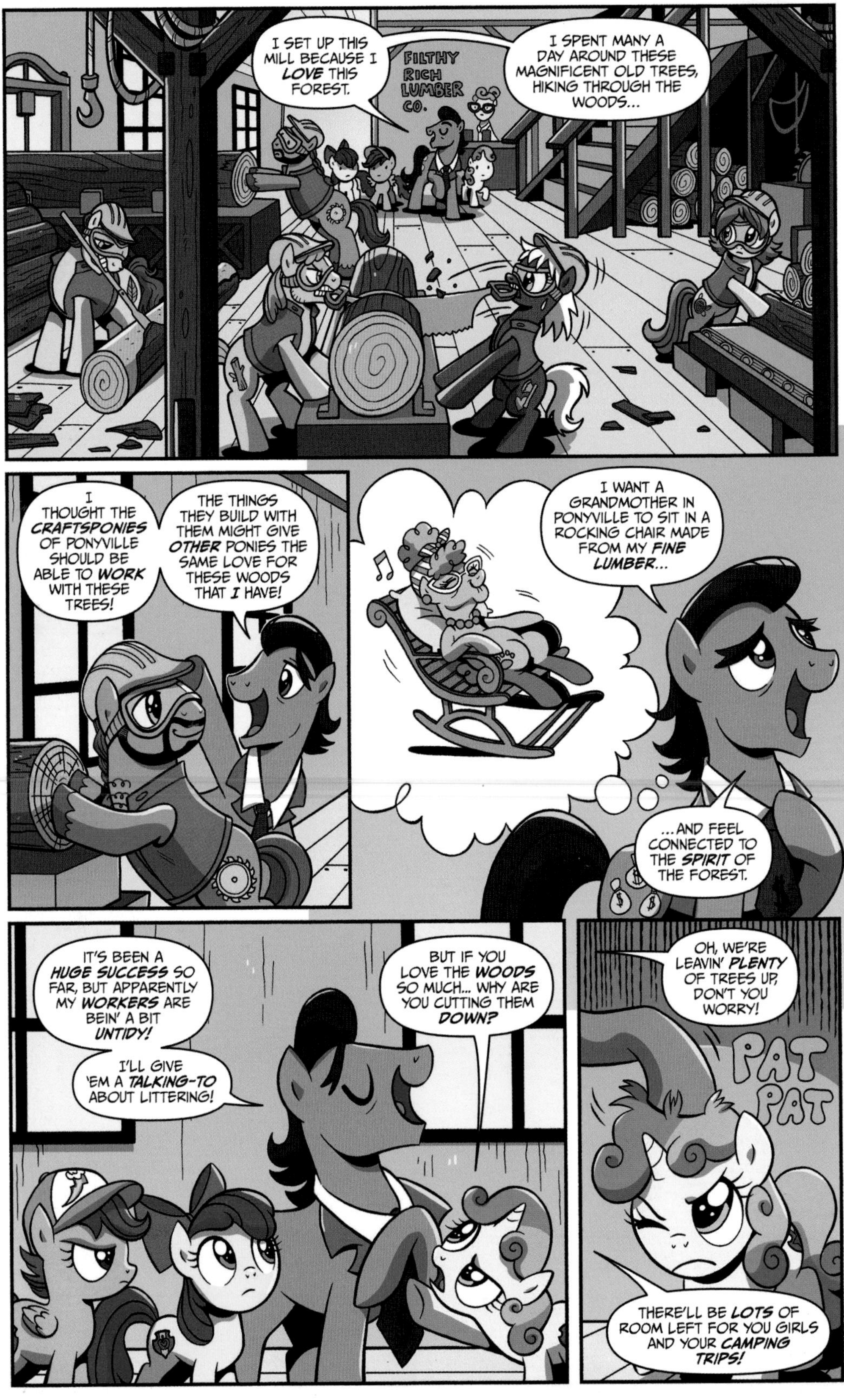
I SET UP THIS MILL BECAUSE I LOVE THIS FOREST.
FILTHY RICH LUMBER CO.
I SPENT MANY A DAY AROUND THESE MAGNIFICENT OLD TREES, HIKING THROUGH THE WOODS...
I THOUGHT THE CRAFTSPONIES OF PONYVILLE SHOULD BE ABLE TO WORK WITH THESE TREES!
THE THINGS THEY BUILD WITH THEM MIGHT GIVE OTHER PONIES THE SAME LOVE FOR THESE WOODS THAT I HAVE!
I WANT A GRANDMOTHER IN PONYVILLE TO SIT IN A ROCKING CHAIR MADE FROM MY FINE LUMBER...
...AND FEEL CONNECTED TO THE SPIRIT OF THE FOREST.
IT'S BEEN A HUGE SUCCESS SO FAR, BUT APPARENTLY MY WORKERS ARE BEIN' A BIT UNTIDY!
I'LL GIVE 'EM A TALKING-TO ABOUT LITTERING!
BUT IF YOU LOVE THE WOODS SO MUCH... WHY ARE YOU CUTTING THEM DOWN?
OH, WE'RE LEAVIN' PLENTY OF TREES UP, DON'T YOU WORRY!
PAT PAT
THERE'LL BE LOTS OF ROOM LEFT FOR YOU GIRLS AND YOUR CAMPING TRIPS!

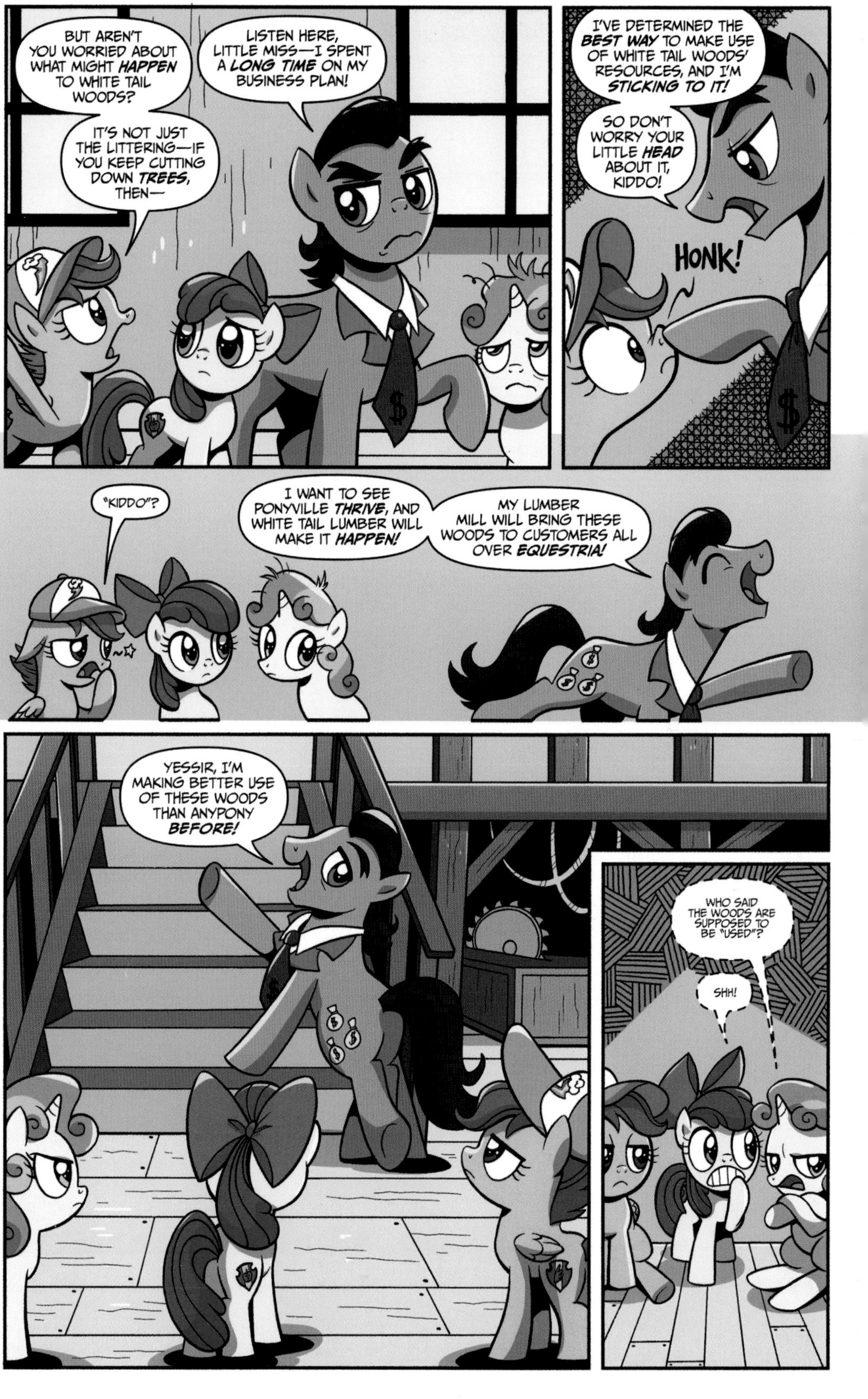
BUT AREN'T YOU WORRIED ABOUT WHAT MIGHT HAPPEN TO WHITE TAIL WOODS?
IT'S NOT JUST THE LITTERING—IF YOU KEEP CUTTING DOWN TREES, THEN—
LISTEN HERE, LITTLE MISS—I SPENT A LONG TIME ON MY BUSINESS PLAN!
I'VE DETERMINED THE BEST WAY TO MAKE USE OF WHITE TAIL WOODS' RESOURCES, AND I'M STICKING TO IT!
SO DON'T WORRY YOUR LITTLE HEAD ABOUT IT, KIDDO!
HONK!
"KIDDO"?
I WANT TO SEE PONYVILLE THRIVE, AND WHITE TAIL LUMBER WILL MAKE IT HAPPEN!
MY LUMBER MILL WILL BRING THESE WOODS TO CUSTOMERS ALL OVER EQUESTRIA!
YESSIR, I'M MAKING BETTER USE OF THESE WOODS THAN ANYPONY BEFORE!
WHO SAID THE WOODS ARE SUPPOSED TO BE "USED"?
SHH!

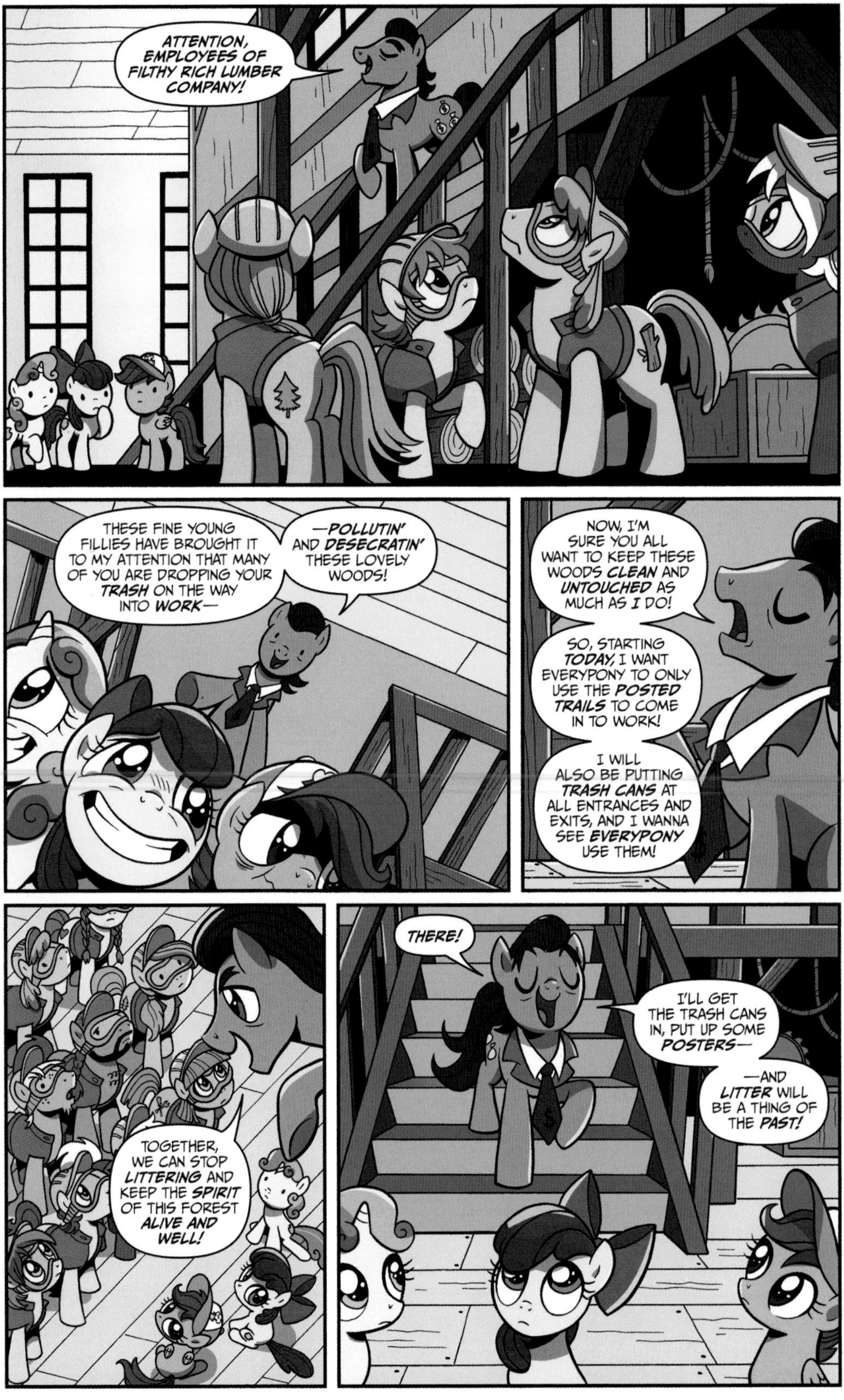
ATTENTION, EMPLOYEES OF FILTHY RICH LUMBER COMPANY!
THESE FINE YOUNG FILLIES HAVE BROUGHT IT TO MY ATTENTION THAT MANY OF YOU ARE DROPPING YOUR TRASH ON THE WAY INTO WORK—
—POLLUTIN' AND DESECRATIN' THESE LOVELY WOODS!
NOW, I'M SURE YOU ALL WANT TO KEEP THESE WOODS CLEAN AND UNTOUCHED AS MUCH AS I DO!
SO, STARTING TODAY, I WANT EVERYPONY TO ONLY USE THE POSTED TRAILS TO COME IN TO WORK!
I WILL ALSO BE PUTTING TRASH CANS AT ALL ENTRANCES AND EXITS, AND I WANNA SEE EVERYPONY USE THEM!
TOGETHER, WE CAN STOP LITTERING AND KEEP THE SPIRIT OF THIS FOREST ALIVE AND WELL!
THERE!
I'LL GET THE TRASH CANS IN, PUT UP SOME POSTERS—
—AND LITTER WILL BE A THING OF THE PAST!

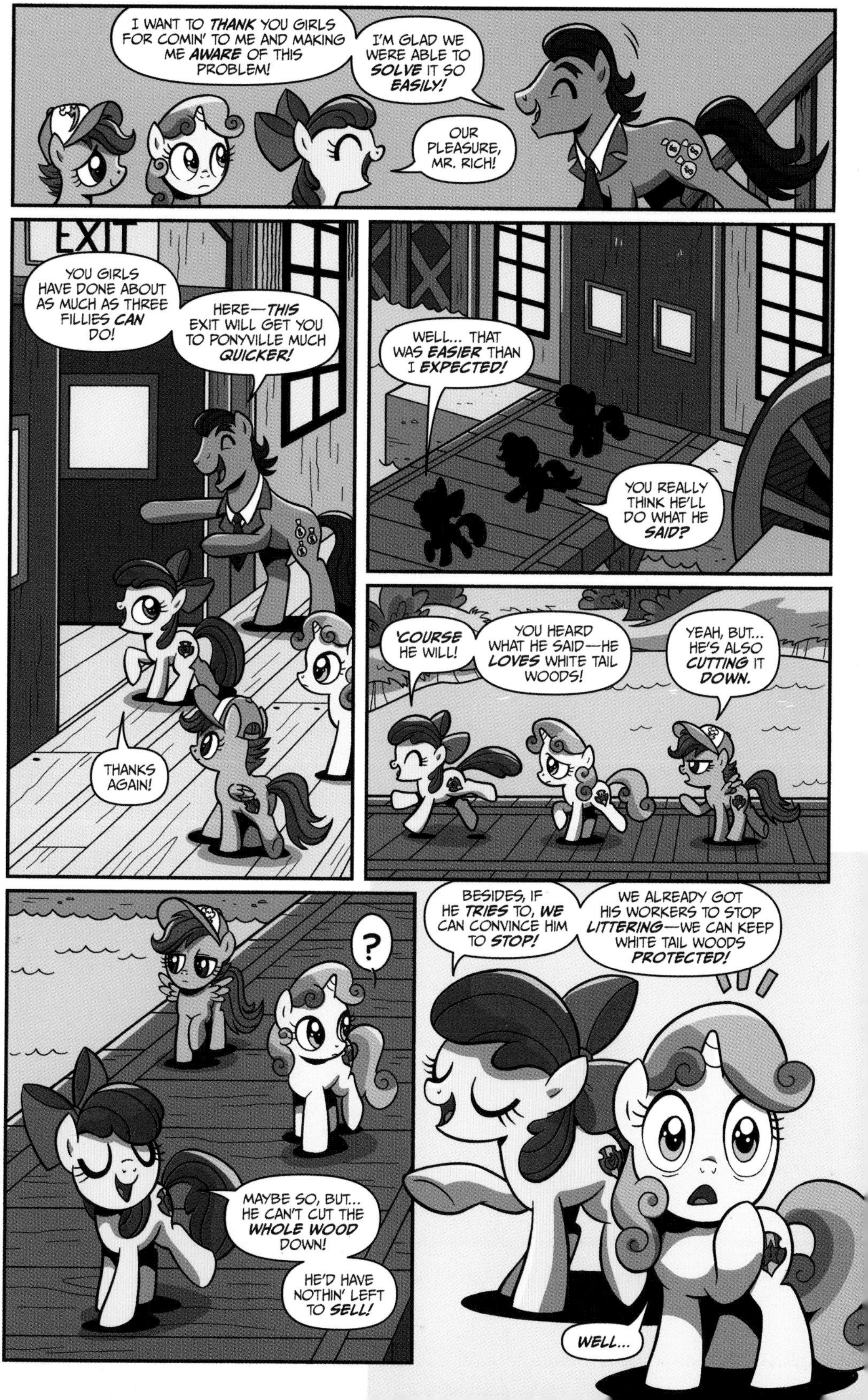
I WANT TO THANK YOU GIRLS FOR COMIN' TO ME AND MAKING ME AWARE OF THIS PROBLEM!
I'M GLAD WE WERE ABLE TO SOLVE IT SO EASILY!
OUR PLEASURE, MR. RICH!
EXIT
YOU GIRLS HAVE DONE ABOUT AS MUCH AS THREE FILLIES CAN DO!
HERE—THIS EXIT WILL GET YOU TO PONYVILLE MUCH QUICKER!
THANKS AGAIN!
WELL... THAT WAS EASIER THAN I EXPECTED!
YOU REALLY THINK HE'LL DO WHAT HE SAID?
'COURSE HE WILL!
YOU HEARD WHAT HE SAID—HE LOVES WHITE TAIL WOODS!
YEAH, BUT... HE'S ALSO CUTTING IT DOWN.
?
MAYBE SO, BUT... HE CAN'T CUT THE WHOLE WOOD DOWN!
HE'D HAVE NOTHIN' LEFT TO SELL!
BESIDES, IF HE TRIES TO, WE CAN CONVINCE HIM TO STOP!
WE ALREADY GOT HIS WORKERS TO STOP LITTERING—WE CAN KEEP WHITE TAIL WOODS PROTECTED!
WELL...

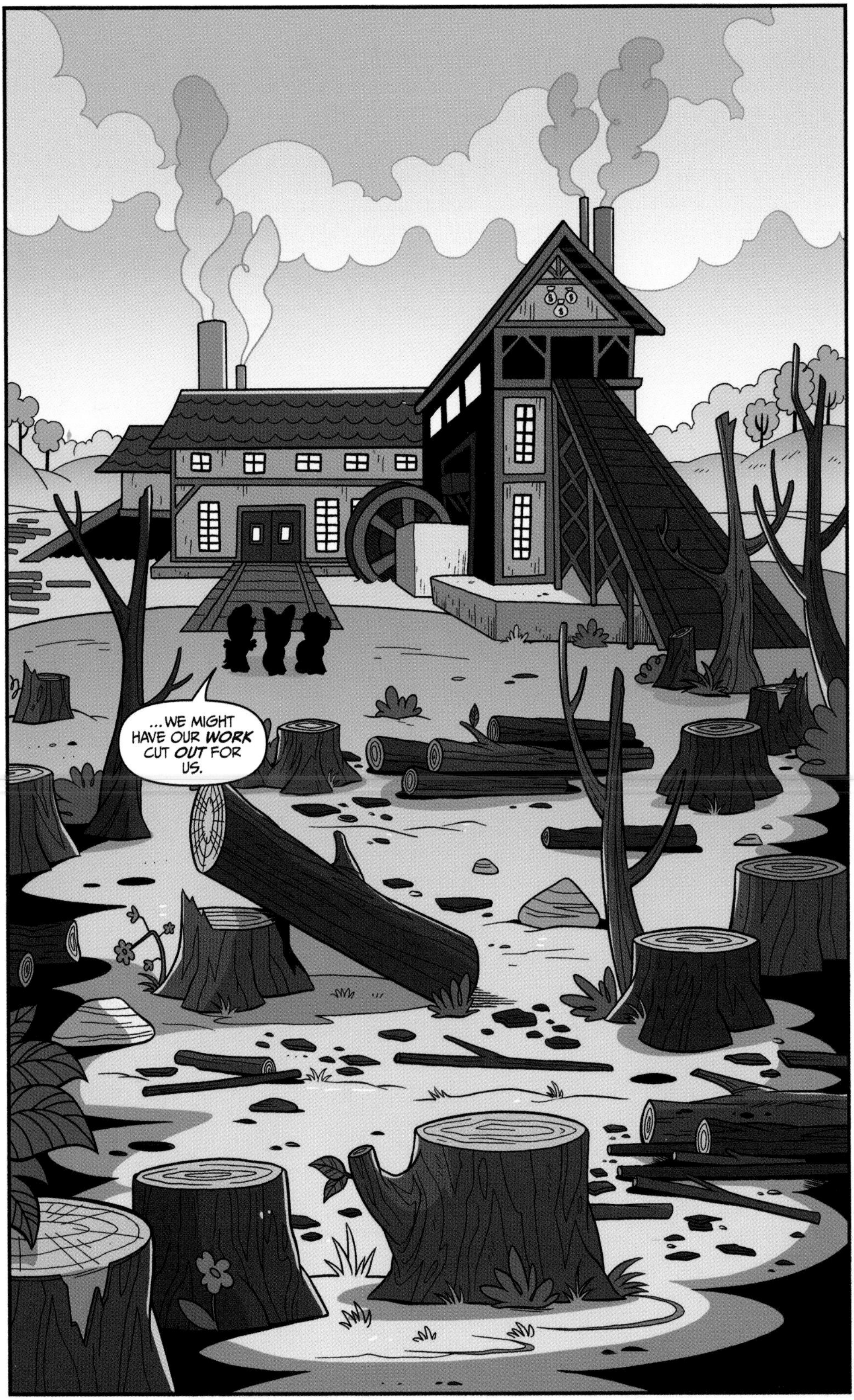
...WE MIGHT HAVE OUR WORK CUT OUT FOR US.

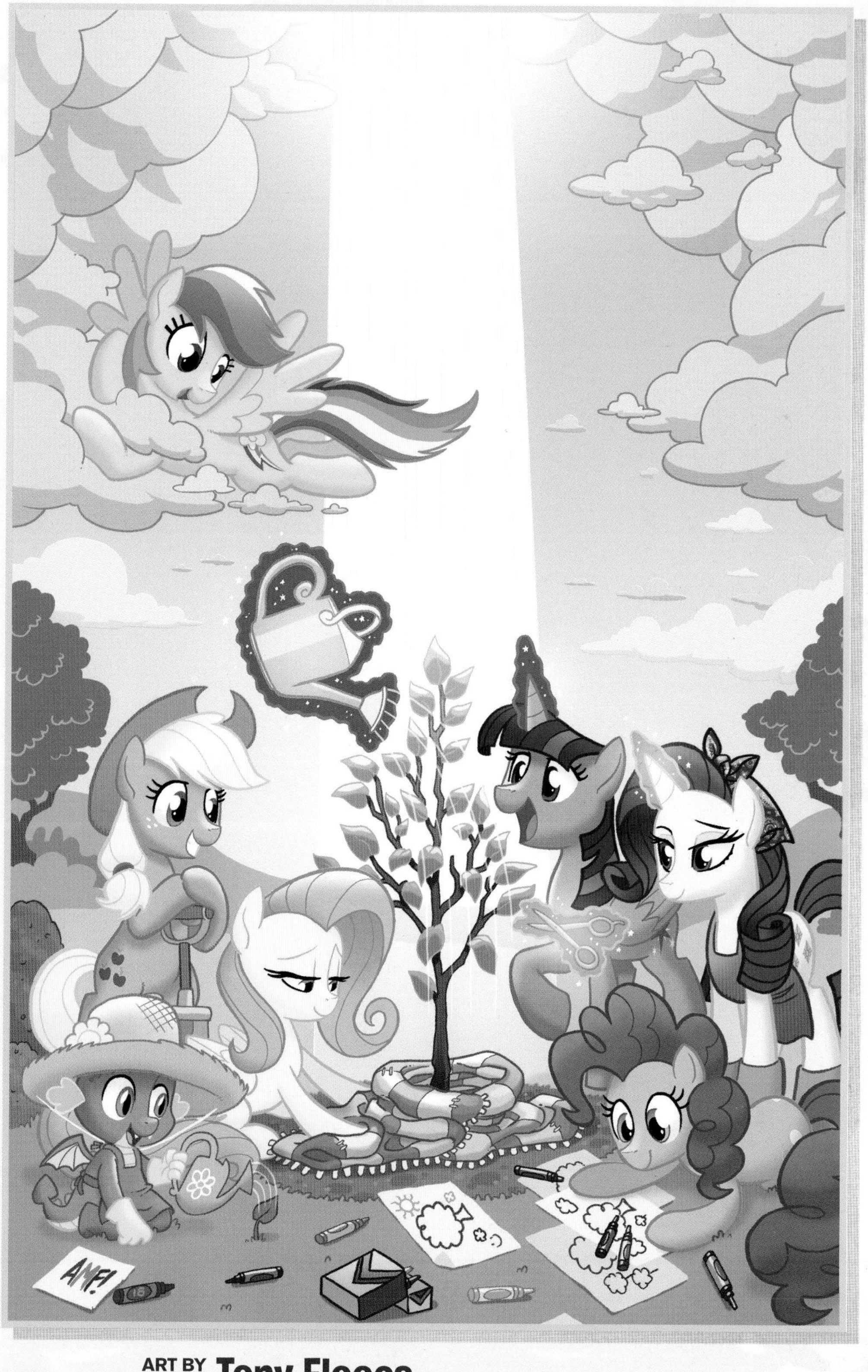
AMF!

ART BY **Tony Fleecs**

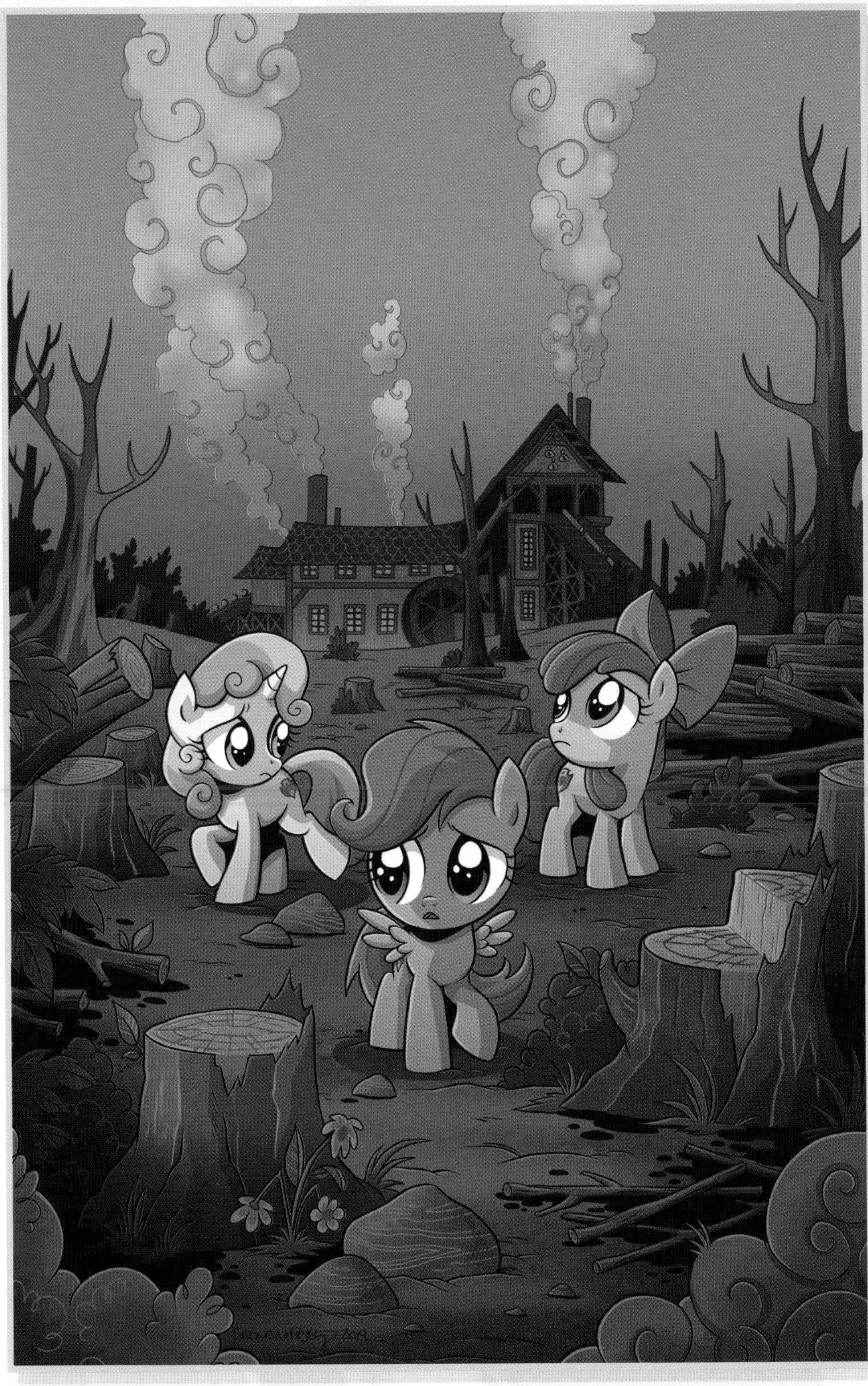

ART BY **Brenda Hickey**

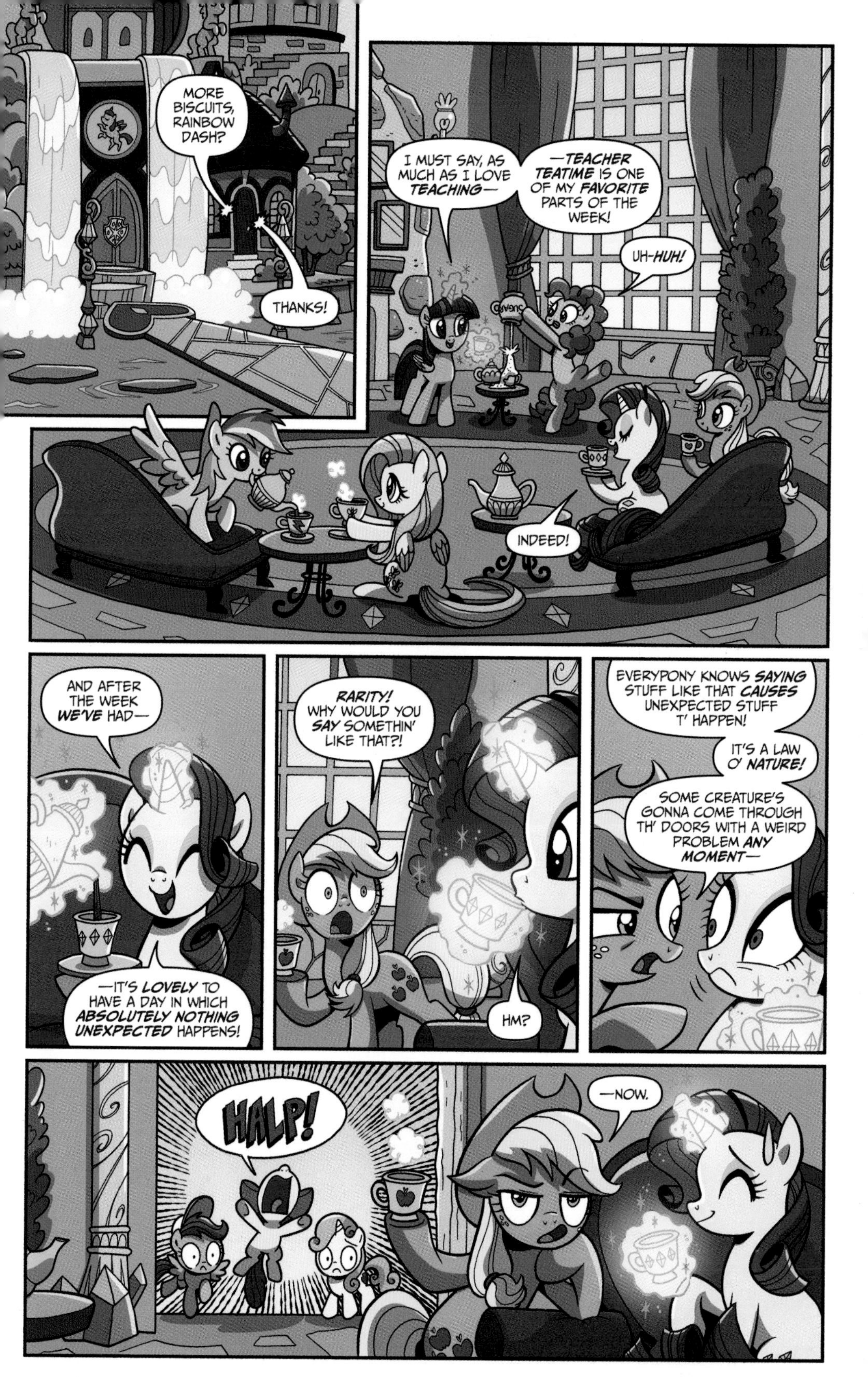
MORE BISCUITS, RAINBOW DASH?
THANKS!
I MUST SAY, AS MUCH AS I LOVE TEACHING—
—TEACHER TEATIME IS ONE OF MY FAVORITE PARTS OF THE WEEK!
UH-HUH!
INDEED!
AND AFTER THE WEEK WE'VE HAD—
—IT'S LOVELY TO HAVE A DAY IN WHICH ABSOLUTELY NOTHING UNEXPECTED HAPPENS!
RARITY! WHY WOULD YOU SAY SOMETHIN' LIKE THAT?!
HM?
EVERYPONY KNOWS SAYING STUFF LIKE THAT CAUSES UNEXPECTED STUFF T' HAPPEN!
IT'S A LAW O' NATURE!
SOME CREATURE'S GONNA COME THROUGH TH' DOORS WITH A WEIRD PROBLEM ANY MOMENT—
HALP!
—NOW.

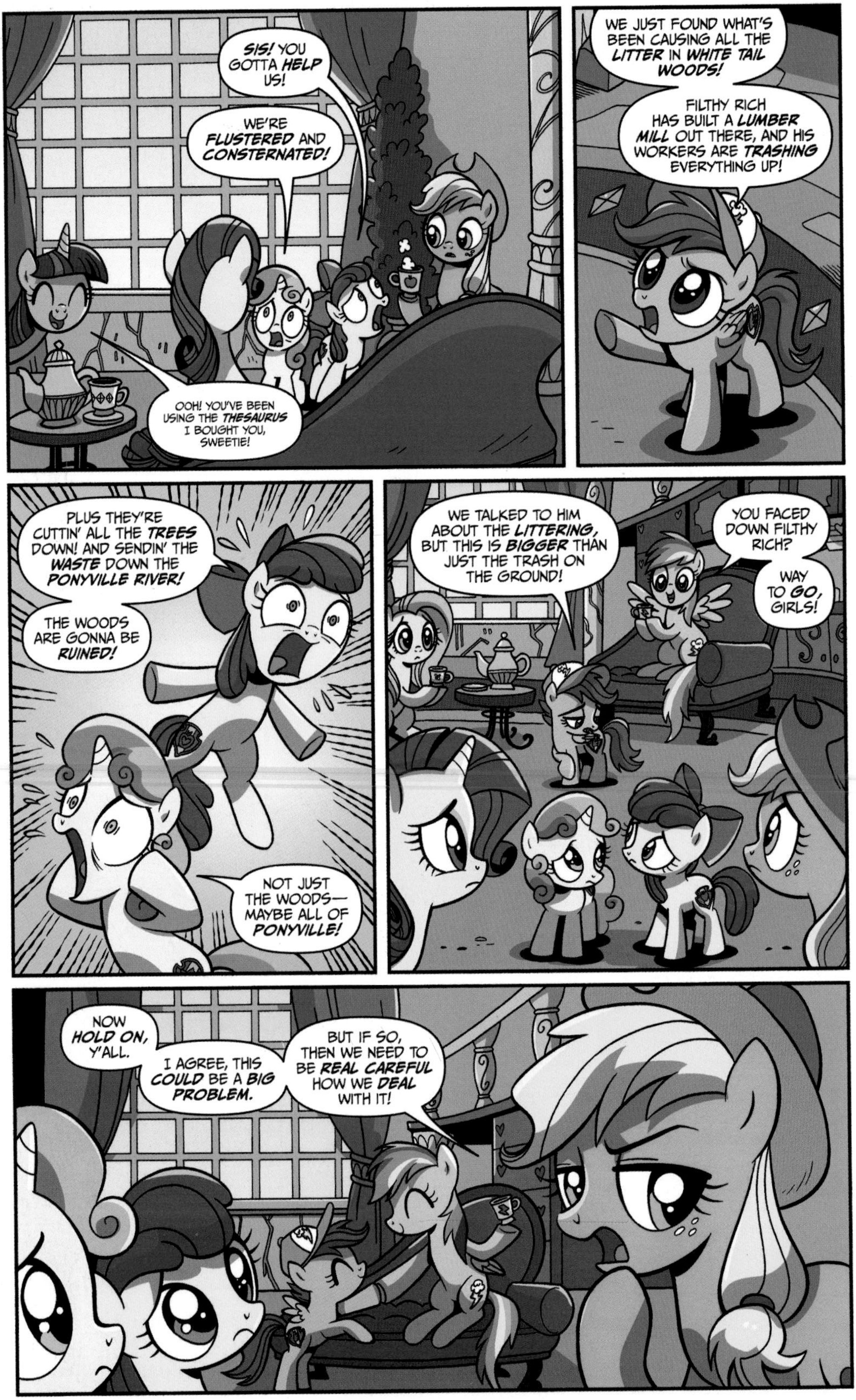
SIS! YOU GOTTA HELP US!
WE'RE FLUSTERED AND CONSTERNATED!
OOH! YOU'VE BEEN USING THE THESAURUS I BOUGHT YOU, SWEETIE!
WE JUST FOUND WHAT'S BEEN CAUSING ALL THE LITTER IN WHITE TAIL WOODS!
FILTHY RICH HAS BUILT A LUMBER MILL OUT THERE, AND HIS WORKERS ARE TRASHING EVERYTHING UP!
PLUS THEY'RE CUTTIN' ALL THE TREES DOWN! AND SENDIN' THE WASTE DOWN THE PONYVILLE RIVER!
THE WOODS ARE GONNA BE RUINED!
NOT JUST THE WOODS— MAYBE ALL OF PONYVILLE!
WE TALKED TO HIM ABOUT THE LITTERING, BUT THIS IS BIGGER THAN JUST THE TRASH ON THE GROUND!
YOU FACED DOWN FILTHY RICH?
WAY TO GO, GIRLS!
NOW HOLD ON, Y'ALL.
I AGREE, THIS COULD BE A BIG PROBLEM.
BUT IF SO, THEN WE NEED TO BE REAL CAREFUL HOW WE DEAL WITH IT!

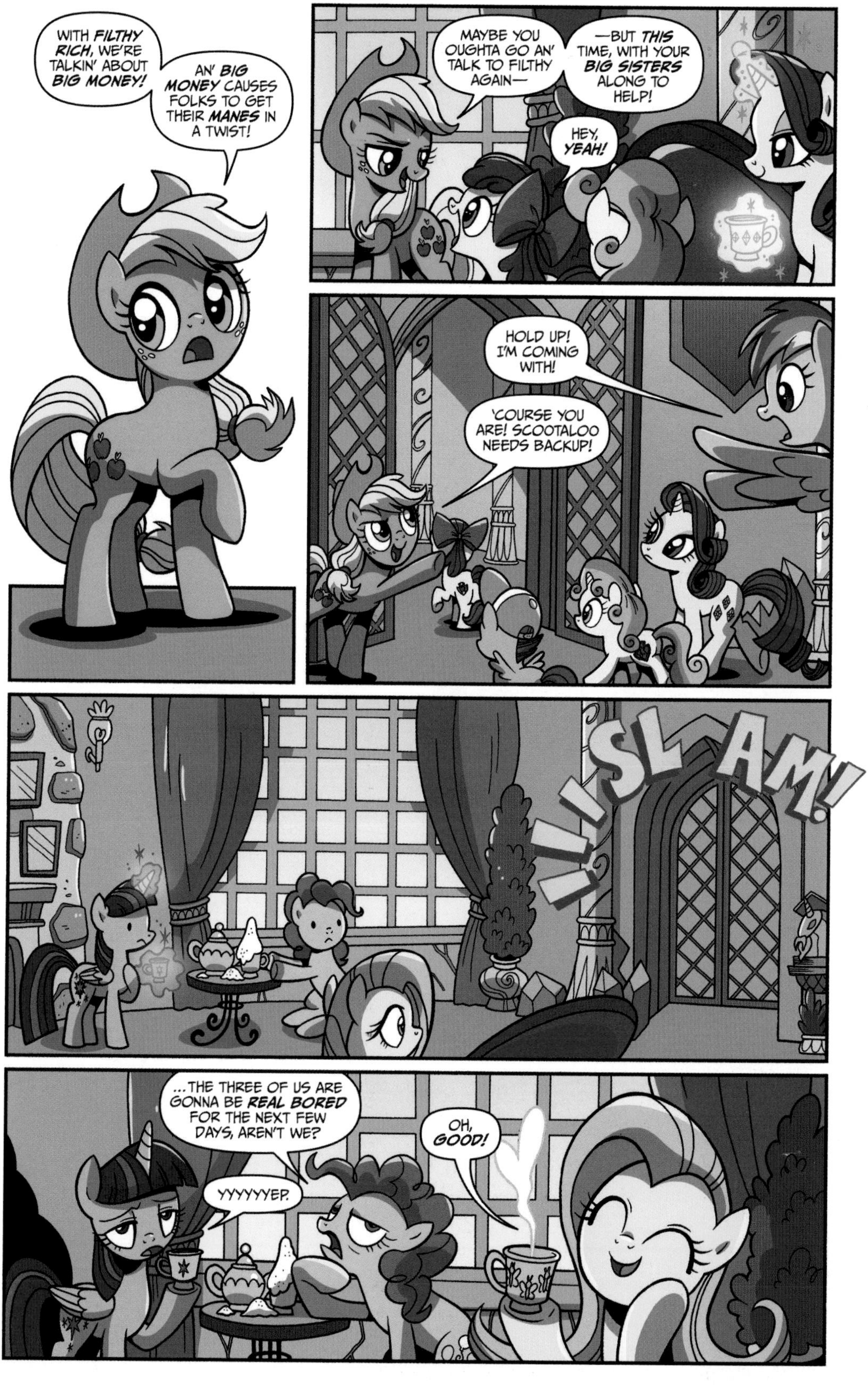

WITH FILTHY RICH, WE'RE TALKIN' ABOUT BIG MONEY!
AN' BIG MONEY CAUSES FOLKS TO GET THEIR MANES IN A TWIST!
MAYBE YOU OUGHTA GO AN' TALK TO FILTHY AGAIN—
—BUT THIS TIME, WITH YOUR BIG SISTERS ALONG TO HELP!
HEY, YEAH!
HOLD UP! I'M COMING WITH!
'COURSE YOU ARE! SCOOTALOO NEEDS BACKUP!
SLAM!
...THE THREE OF US ARE GONNA BE REAL BORED FOR THE NEXT FEW DAYS, AREN'T WE?
YYYYYYEP.
OH, GOOD!

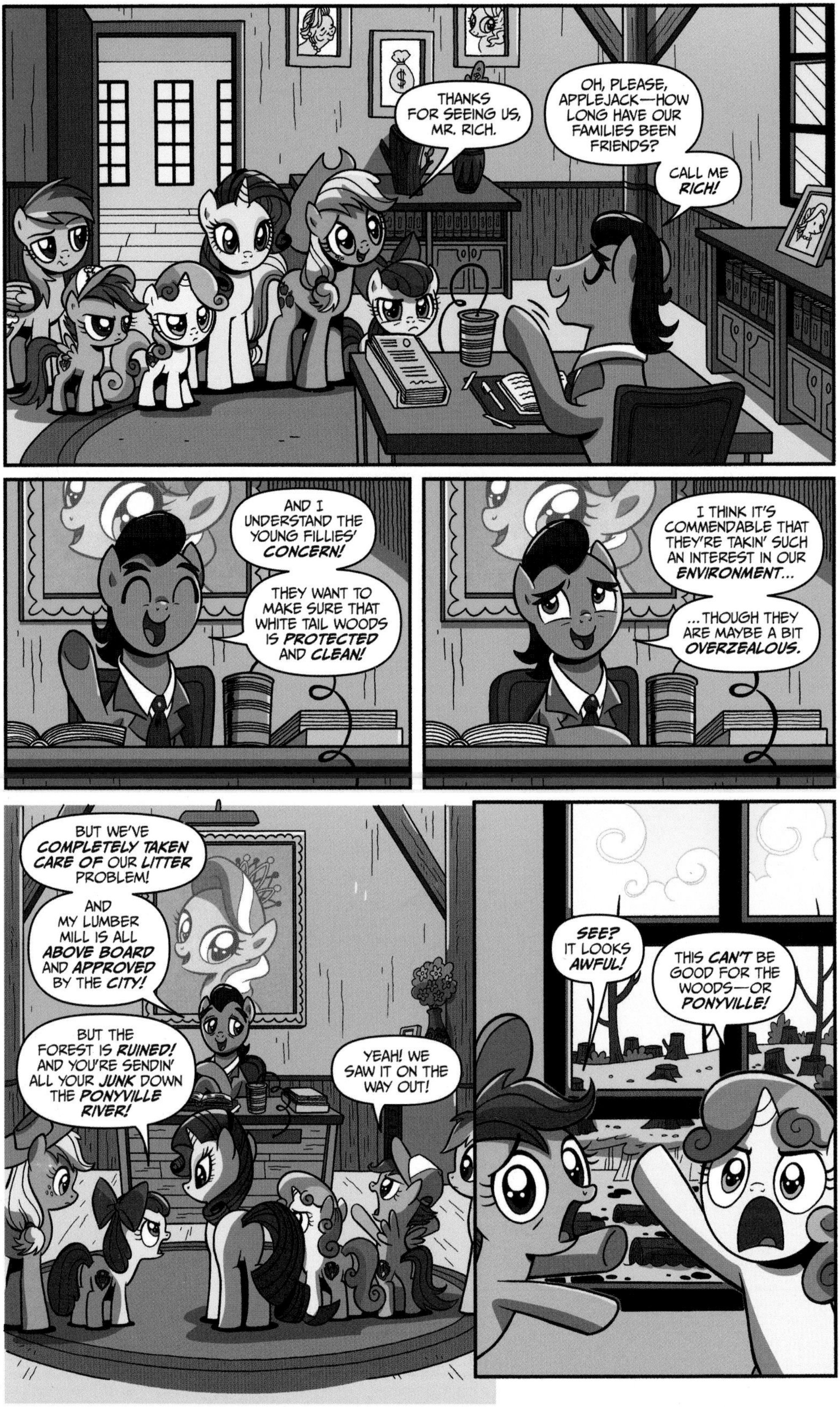
THANKS FOR SEEING US, MR. RICH.
OH, PLEASE, APPLEJACK—HOW LONG HAVE OUR FAMILIES BEEN FRIENDS?
CALL ME RICH!
AND I UNDERSTAND THE YOUNG FILLIES' CONCERN!
THEY WANT TO MAKE SURE THAT WHITE TAIL WOODS IS PROTECTED AND CLEAN!
I THINK IT'S COMMENDABLE THAT THEY'RE TAKIN' SUCH AN INTEREST IN OUR ENVIRONMENT...
...THOUGH THEY ARE MAYBE A BIT OVERZEALOUS.
BUT WE'VE COMPLETELY TAKEN CARE OF OUR LITTER PROBLEM!
AND MY LUMBER MILL IS ALL ABOVE BOARD AND APPROVED BY THE CITY!
BUT THE FOREST IS RUINED! AND YOU'RE SENDIN' ALL YOUR JUNK DOWN THE PONYVILLE RIVER!
YEAH! WE SAW IT ON THE WAY OUT!
SEE? IT LOOKS AWFUL!
THIS CAN'T BE GOOD FOR THE WOODS—OR PONYVILLE!

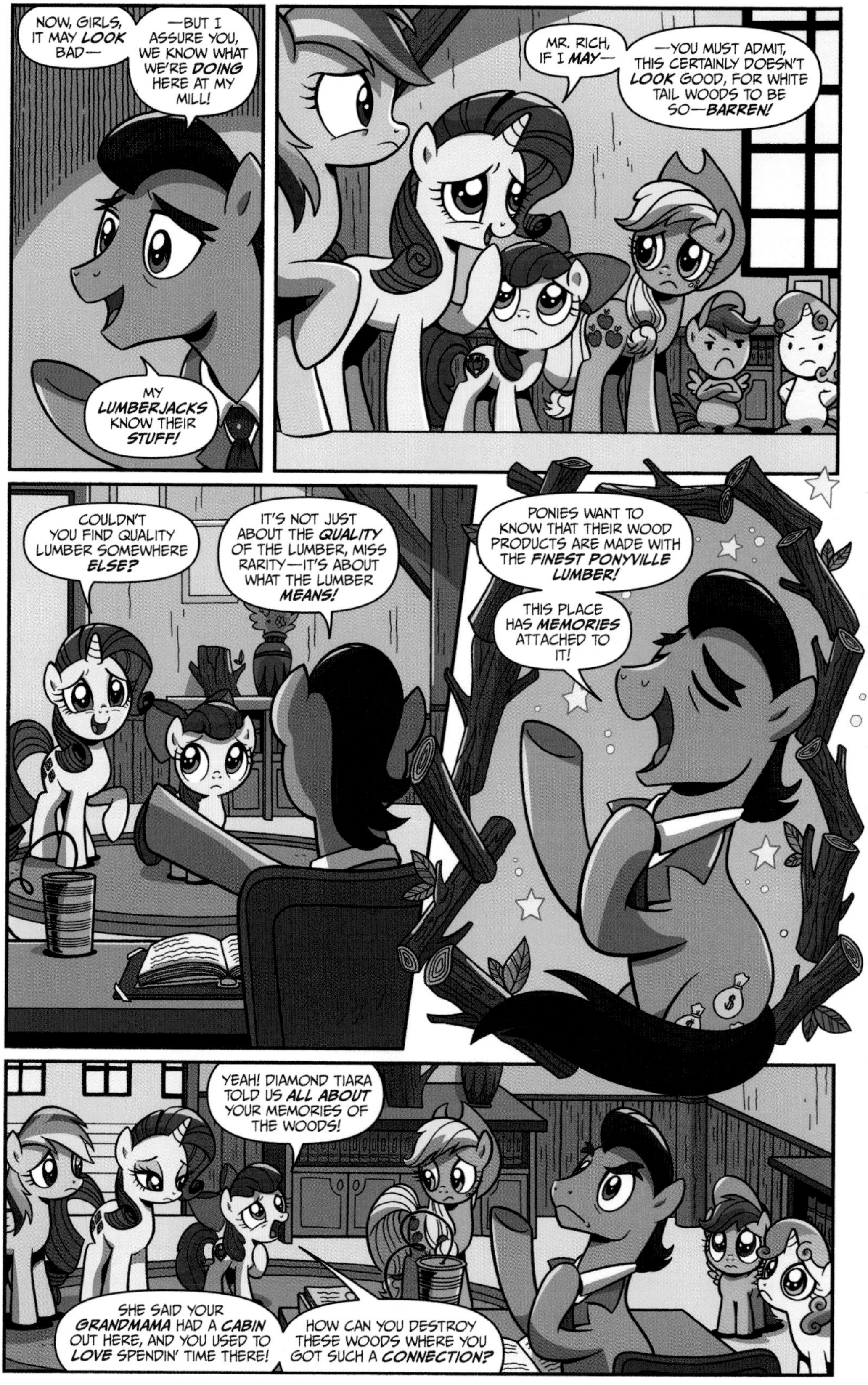
NOW, GIRLS, IT MAY *LOOK* BAD—
—BUT I ASSURE YOU, WE KNOW WHAT WE'RE *DOING* HERE AT MY MILL!
MY *LUMBERJACKS* KNOW THEIR *STUFF!*
MR. RICH, IF I *MAY*—
—YOU MUST ADMIT, THIS CERTAINLY DOESN'T *LOOK* GOOD, FOR WHITE TAIL WOODS TO BE SO—*BARREN!*
COULDN'T YOU FIND QUALITY LUMBER SOMEWHERE *ELSE?*
IT'S NOT JUST ABOUT THE *QUALITY* OF THE LUMBER, MISS RARITY—IT'S ABOUT WHAT THE LUMBER *MEANS!*
PONIES WANT TO KNOW THAT THEIR WOOD PRODUCTS ARE MADE WITH THE *FINEST PONYVILLE LUMBER!*
THIS PLACE HAS *MEMORIES* ATTACHED TO IT!
YEAH! DIAMOND TIARA TOLD US *ALL ABOUT* YOUR MEMORIES OF THE WOODS!
SHE SAID YOUR *GRANDMAMA* HAD A *CABIN* OUT HERE, AND YOU USED TO *LOVE* SPENDIN' TIME THERE!
HOW CAN YOU DESTROY THESE WOODS WHERE YOU GOT SUCH A *CONNECTION?*

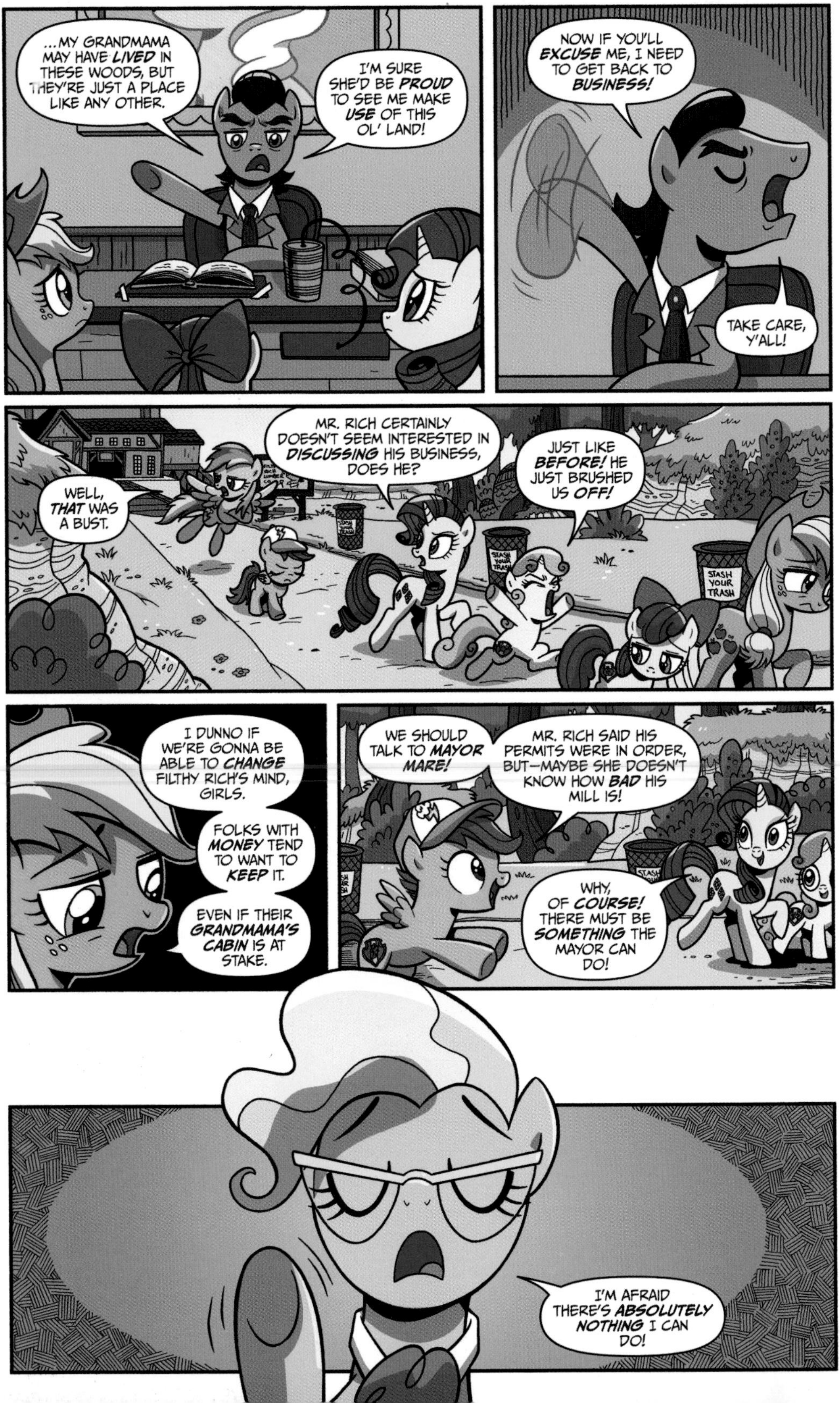
...MY GRANDMAMA MAY HAVE *LIVED* IN THESE WOODS, BUT THEY'RE JUST A PLACE LIKE ANY OTHER.
I'M SURE SHE'D BE *PROUD* TO SEE ME MAKE *USE* OF THIS OL' LAND!
NOW IF YOU'LL *EXCUSE* ME, I NEED TO GET BACK TO *BUSINESS!*
TAKE CARE, Y'ALL!
WELL, *THAT* WAS A BUST.
MR. RICH CERTAINLY DOESN'T SEEM INTERESTED IN *DISCUSSING* HIS BUSINESS, DOES HE?
JUST LIKE *BEFORE!* HE JUST BRUSHED US *OFF!*
STASH YOUR TRASH
I DUNNO IF WE'RE GONNA BE ABLE TO *CHANGE* FILTHY RICH'S MIND, GIRLS.
FOLKS WITH *MONEY* TEND TO WANT TO *KEEP* IT.
EVEN IF THEIR *GRANDMAMA'S CABIN* IS AT STAKE.
WE SHOULD TALK TO *MAYOR MARE!*
MR. RICH SAID HIS PERMITS WERE IN ORDER, BUT—MAYBE SHE DOESN'T KNOW HOW *BAD* HIS MILL IS!
WHY, OF *COURSE!* THERE MUST BE *SOMETHING* THE MAYOR CAN DO!
I'M AFRAID THERE'S *ABSOLUTELY NOTHING* I CAN DO!

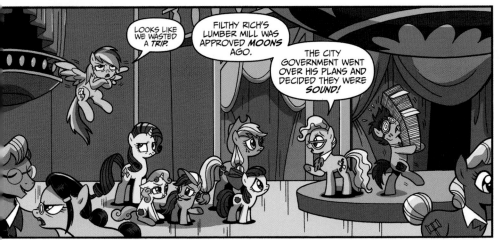

LOOKS LIKE WE WASTED A *TRIP.*

FILTHY RICH'S LUMBER MILL WAS APPROVED *MOONS* AGO.

THE CITY GOVERNMENT WENT OVER HIS PLANS AND DECIDED THEY WERE *SOUND!*

AND TO BE HONEST, THE MILL HAS BEEN GOOD TO PONYVILLE.

HIS LUMBER IS USED BY *MANY* LOCAL BUSINESSES—MAKING *FURNITURE, HOUSES,* ALL *SORTS* OF THINGS!

I UNDERSTAND THAT HIS MILL IS HAVING AN *EFFECT* ON WHITE TAIL WOODS...

...BUT HE ISN'T DOING ANYTHING *WRONG.*

SO THERE'S *NOTHIN'* WE CAN *DO?*

UNFORTUNATELY, *NO.*

BUT IF YOU'RE INTERESTED IN GETTING INVOLVED IN *LOCAL GOVERNMENT...*

...I HAVE SOME *PAMPHLETS* YOU MIGHT—

YOINK

THANKS, MAYOR, BUT WE'LL BE ON OUR *WAY* NOW.

...NOPONY *EVER* WANTS TO SEE THE PAMPHLETS.

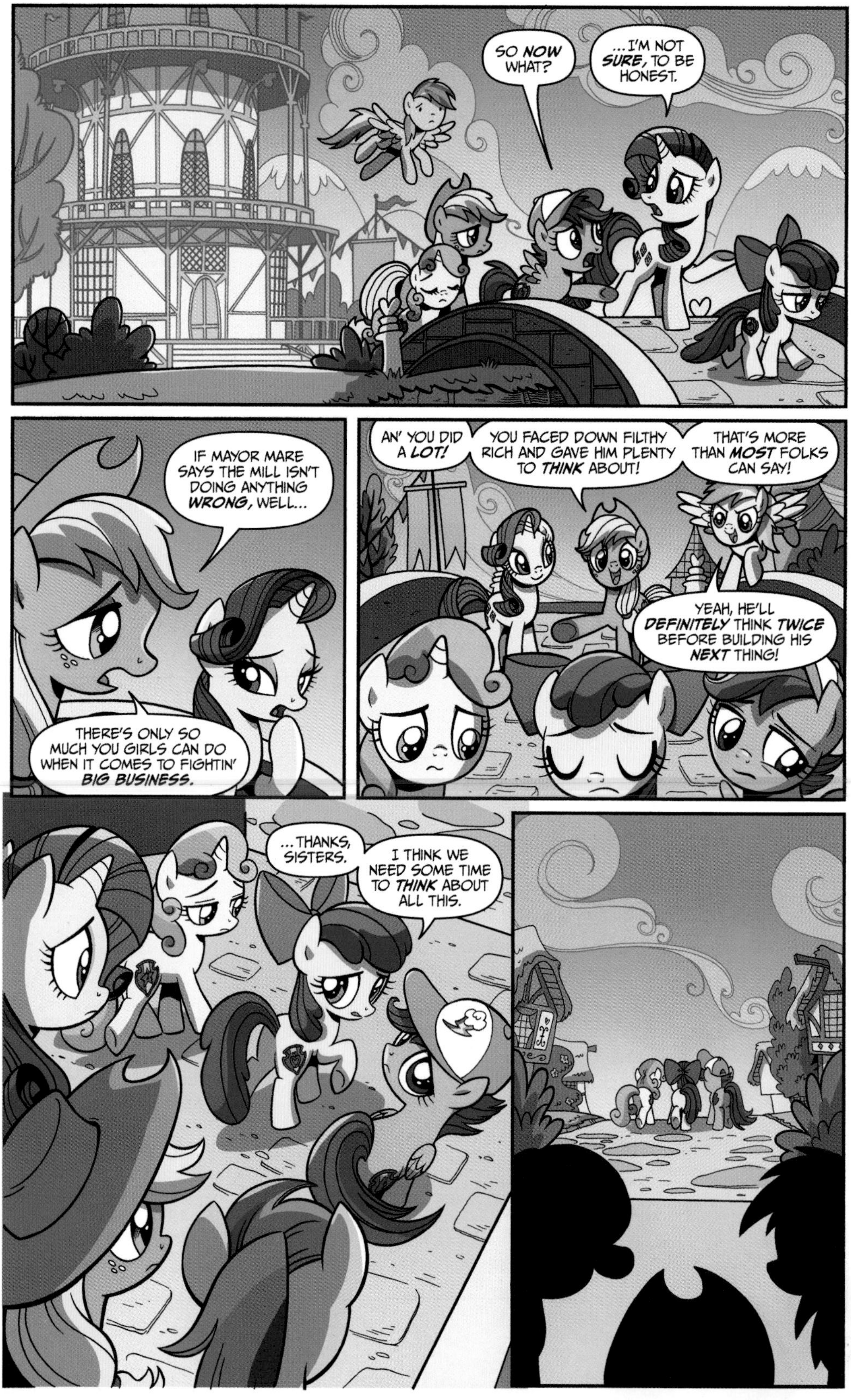
SO NOW WHAT?
...I'M NOT SURE, TO BE HONEST.
IF MAYOR MARE SAYS THE MILL ISN'T DOING ANYTHING WRONG, WELL...
THERE'S ONLY SO MUCH YOU GIRLS CAN DO WHEN IT COMES TO FIGHTIN' BIG BUSINESS.
AN' YOU DID A LOT!
YOU FACED DOWN FILTHY RICH AND GAVE HIM PLENTY TO THINK ABOUT!
THAT'S MORE THAN MOST FOLKS CAN SAY!
YEAH, HE'LL DEFINITELY THINK TWICE BEFORE BUILDING HIS NEXT THING!
...THANKS, SISTERS.
I THINK WE NEED SOME TIME TO THINK ABOUT ALL THIS.

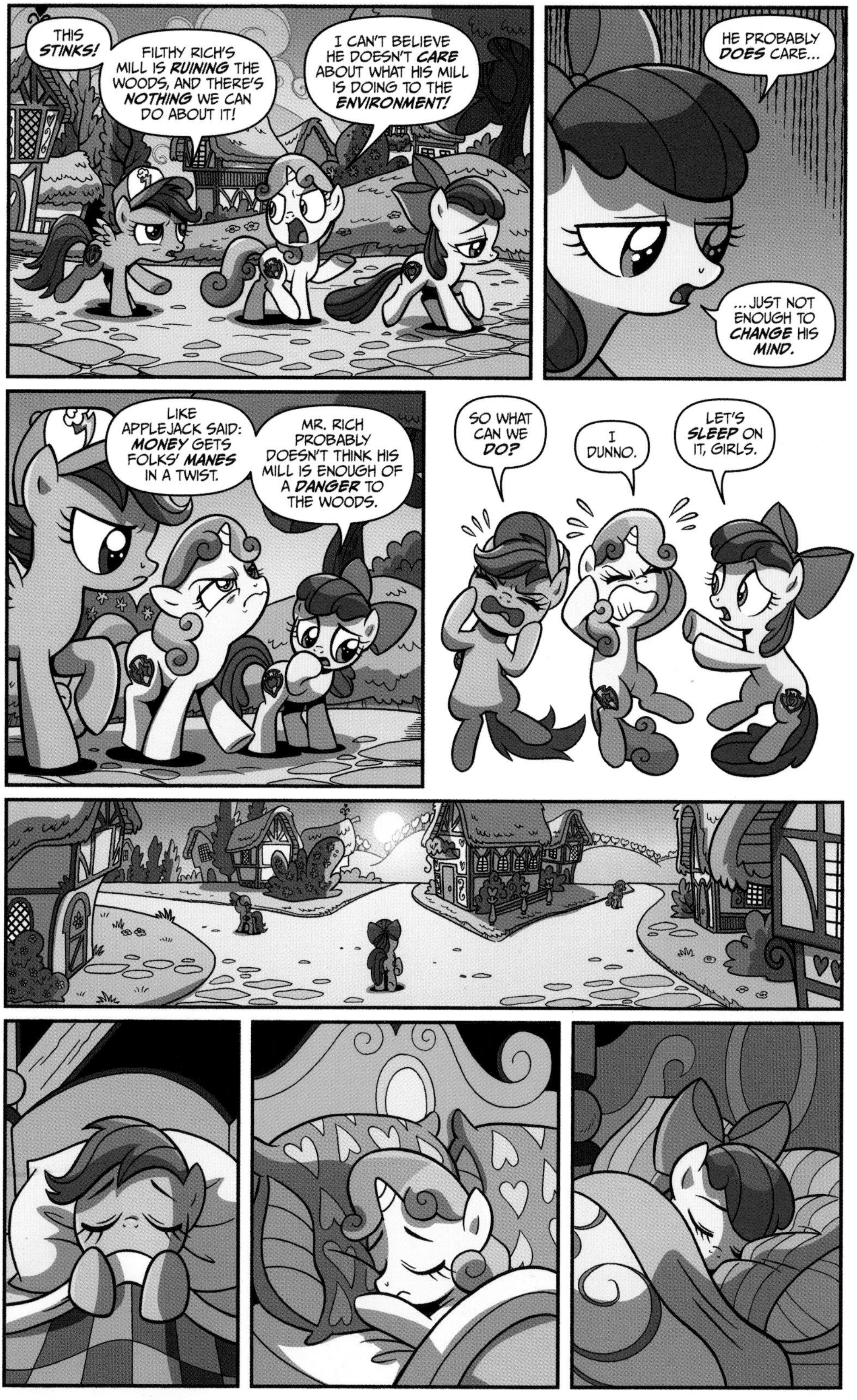
THIS STINKS!
FILTHY RICH'S MILL IS RUINING THE WOODS, AND THERE'S NOTHING WE CAN DO ABOUT IT!
I CAN'T BELIEVE HE DOESN'T CARE ABOUT WHAT HIS MILL IS DOING TO THE ENVIRONMENT!
HE PROBABLY DOES CARE...
...JUST NOT ENOUGH TO CHANGE HIS MIND.
LIKE APPLEJACK SAID: MONEY GETS FOLKS' MANES IN A TWIST.
MR. RICH PROBABLY DOESN'T THINK HIS MILL IS ENOUGH OF A DANGER TO THE WOODS.
SO WHAT CAN WE DO?
I DUNNO.
LET'S SLEEP ON IT, GIRLS.

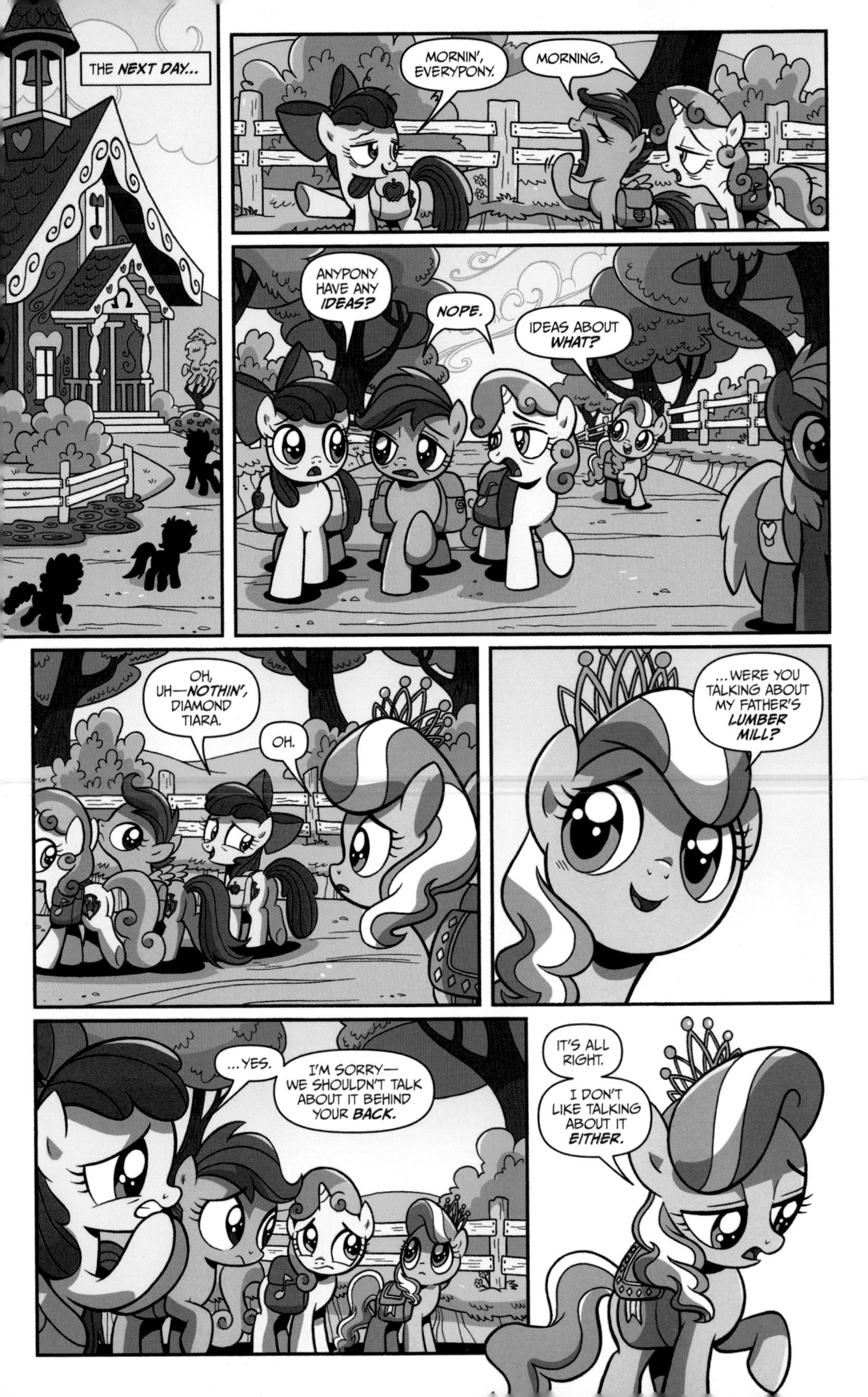
THE NEXT DAY...
MORNIN', EVERYPONY.
MORNING.
ANYPONY HAVE ANY IDEAS?
NOPE.
IDEAS ABOUT WHAT?
OH, UH—NOTHIN', DIAMOND TIARA.
OH.
...WERE YOU TALKING ABOUT MY FATHER'S LUMBER MILL?
...YES.
I'M SORRY— WE SHOULDN'T TALK ABOUT IT BEHIND YOUR BACK.
IT'S ALL RIGHT.
I DON'T LIKE TALKING ABOUT IT EITHER.

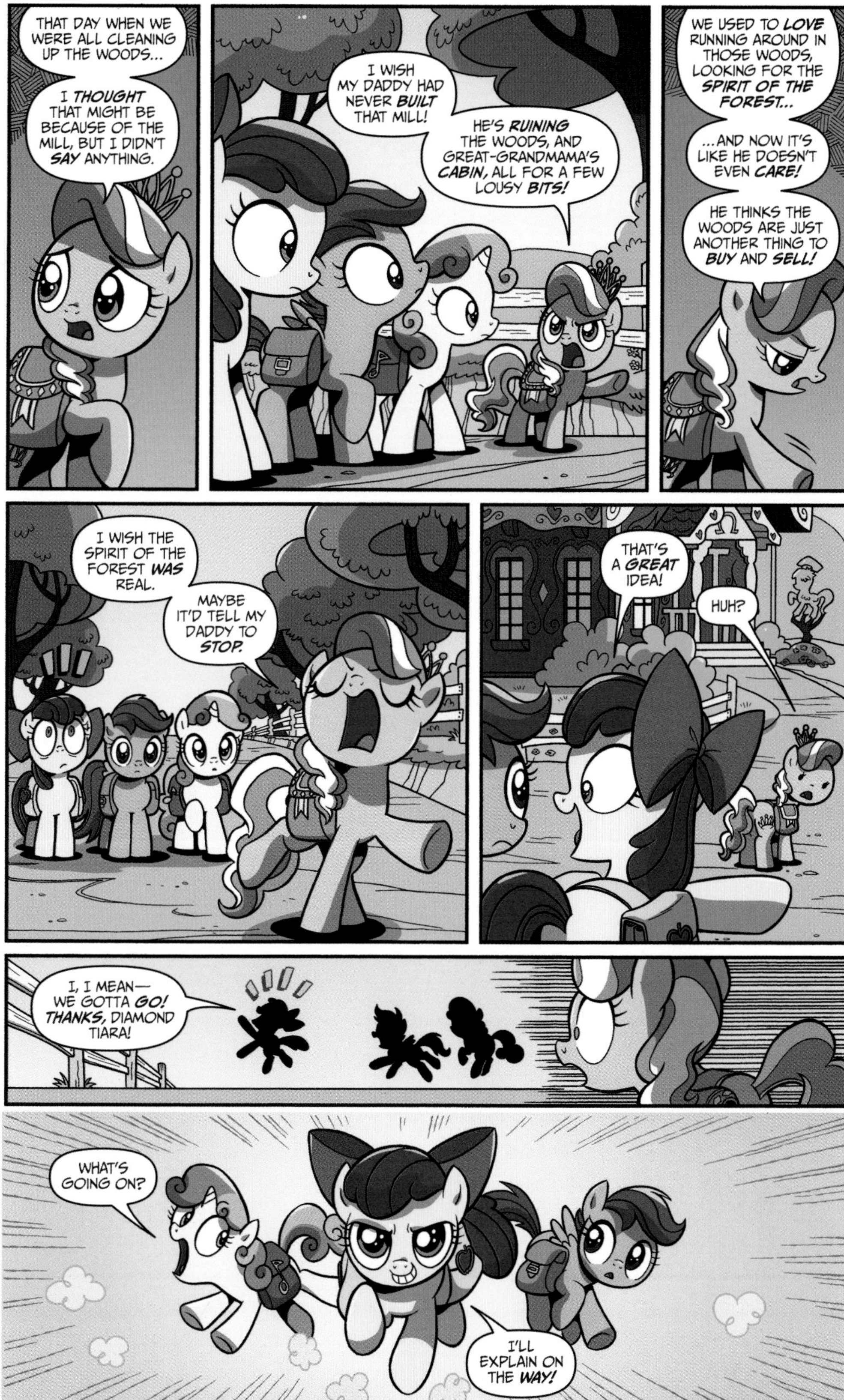
THAT DAY WHEN WE WERE ALL CLEANING UP THE WOODS...
I THOUGHT THAT MIGHT BE BECAUSE OF THE MILL, BUT I DIDN'T SAY ANYTHING.
I WISH MY DADDY HAD NEVER BUILT THAT MILL!
HE'S RUINING THE WOODS, AND GREAT-GRANDMAMA'S CABIN, ALL FOR A FEW LOUSY BITS!
WE USED TO LOVE RUNNING AROUND IN THOSE WOODS, LOOKING FOR THE SPIRIT OF THE FOREST...
...AND NOW IT'S LIKE HE DOESN'T EVEN CARE!
HE THINKS THE WOODS ARE JUST ANOTHER THING TO BUY AND SELL!
I WISH THE SPIRIT OF THE FOREST WAS REAL.
MAYBE IT'D TELL MY DADDY TO STOP.
THAT'S A GREAT IDEA!
HUH?
I, I MEAN— WE GOTTA GO! THANKS, DIAMOND TIARA!
WHAT'S GOING ON?
I'LL EXPLAIN ON THE WAY!

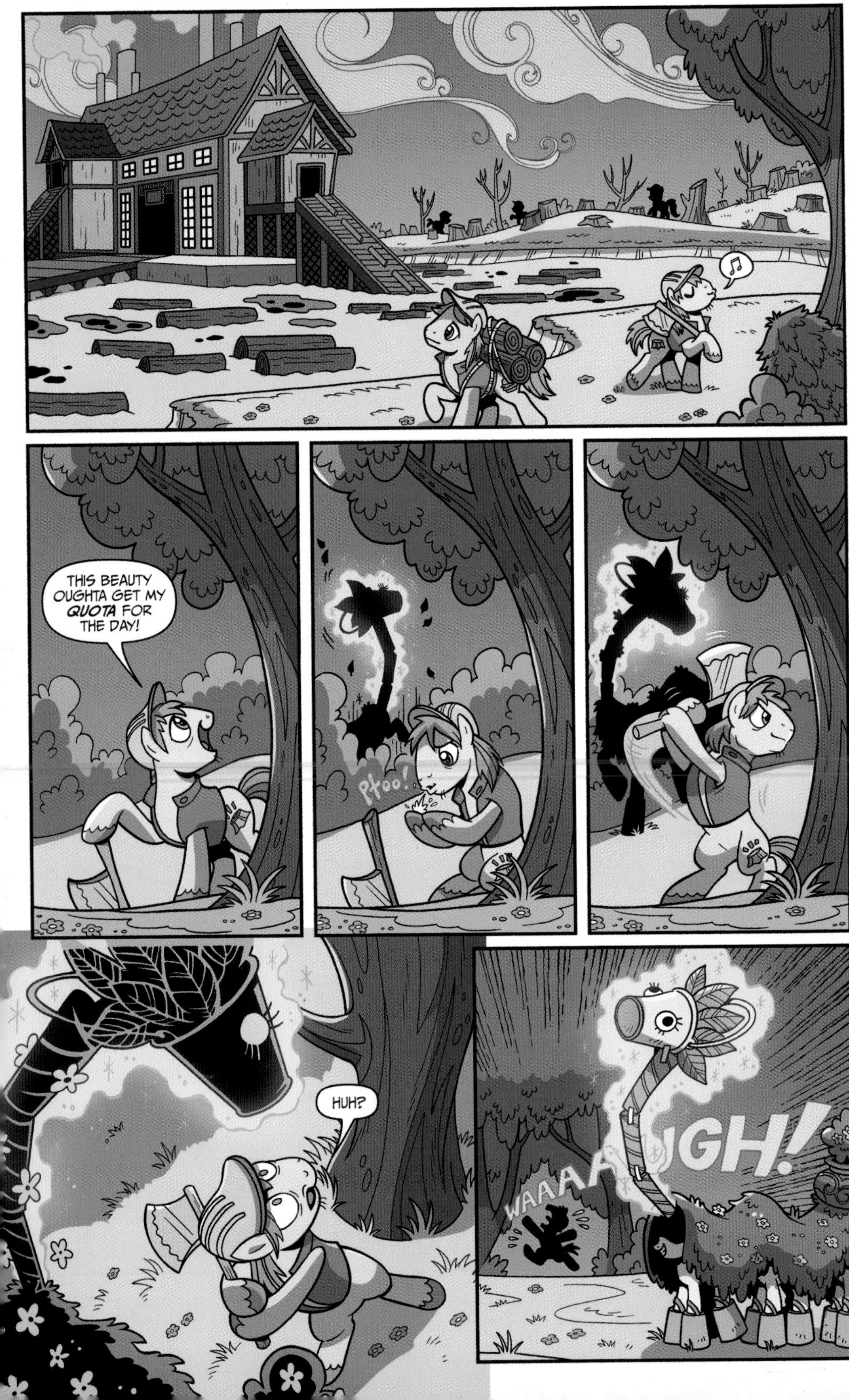
♫
THIS BEAUTY OUGHTA GET MY *QUOTA* FOR THE DAY!
PTOO!
HUH?
WAAAAUGH!

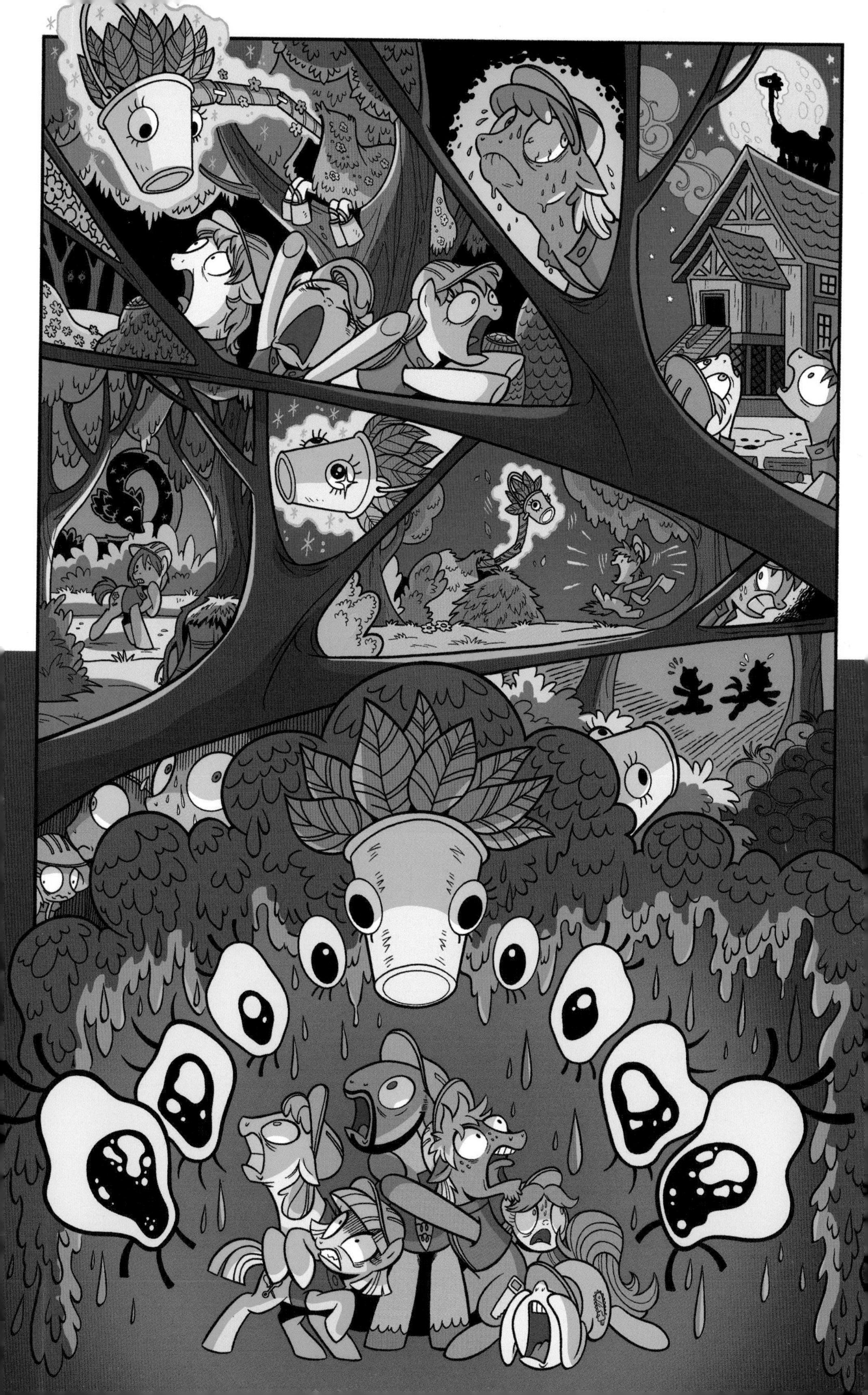

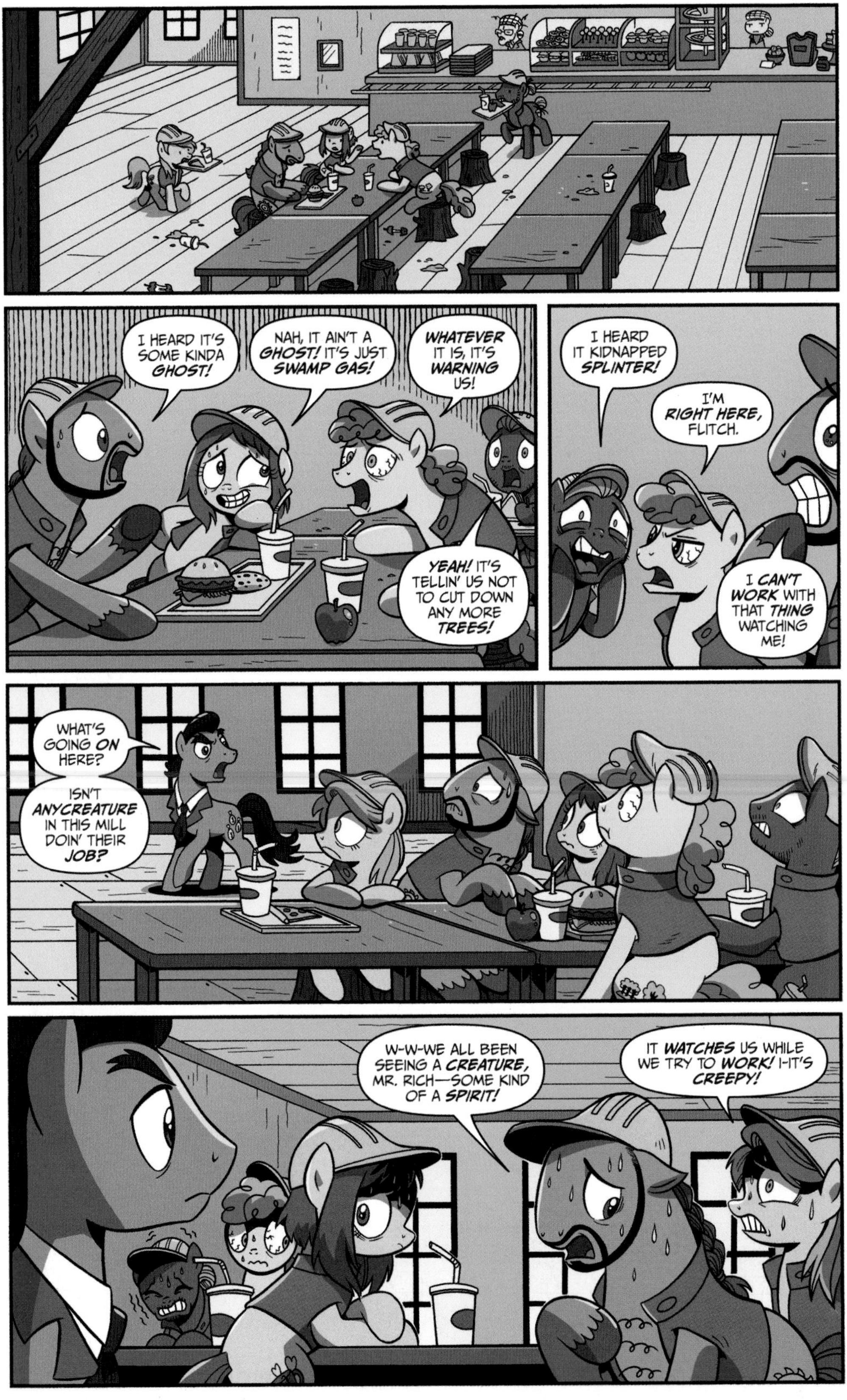
I HEARD IT'S SOME KINDA GHOST!
NAH, IT AIN'T A GHOST! IT'S JUST SWAMP GAS!
WHATEVER IT IS, IT'S WARNING US!
YEAH! IT'S TELLIN' US NOT TO CUT DOWN ANY MORE TREES!
I HEARD IT KIDNAPPED SPLINTER!
I'M RIGHT HERE, FLITCH.
I CAN'T WORK WITH THAT THING WATCHING ME!
WHAT'S GOING ON HERE?
ISN'T ANYCREATURE IN THIS MILL DOIN' THEIR JOB?
W-W-WE ALL BEEN SEEING A CREATURE, MR. RICH—SOME KIND OF A SPIRIT!
IT WATCHES US WHILE WE TRY TO WORK! I-IT'S CREEPY!

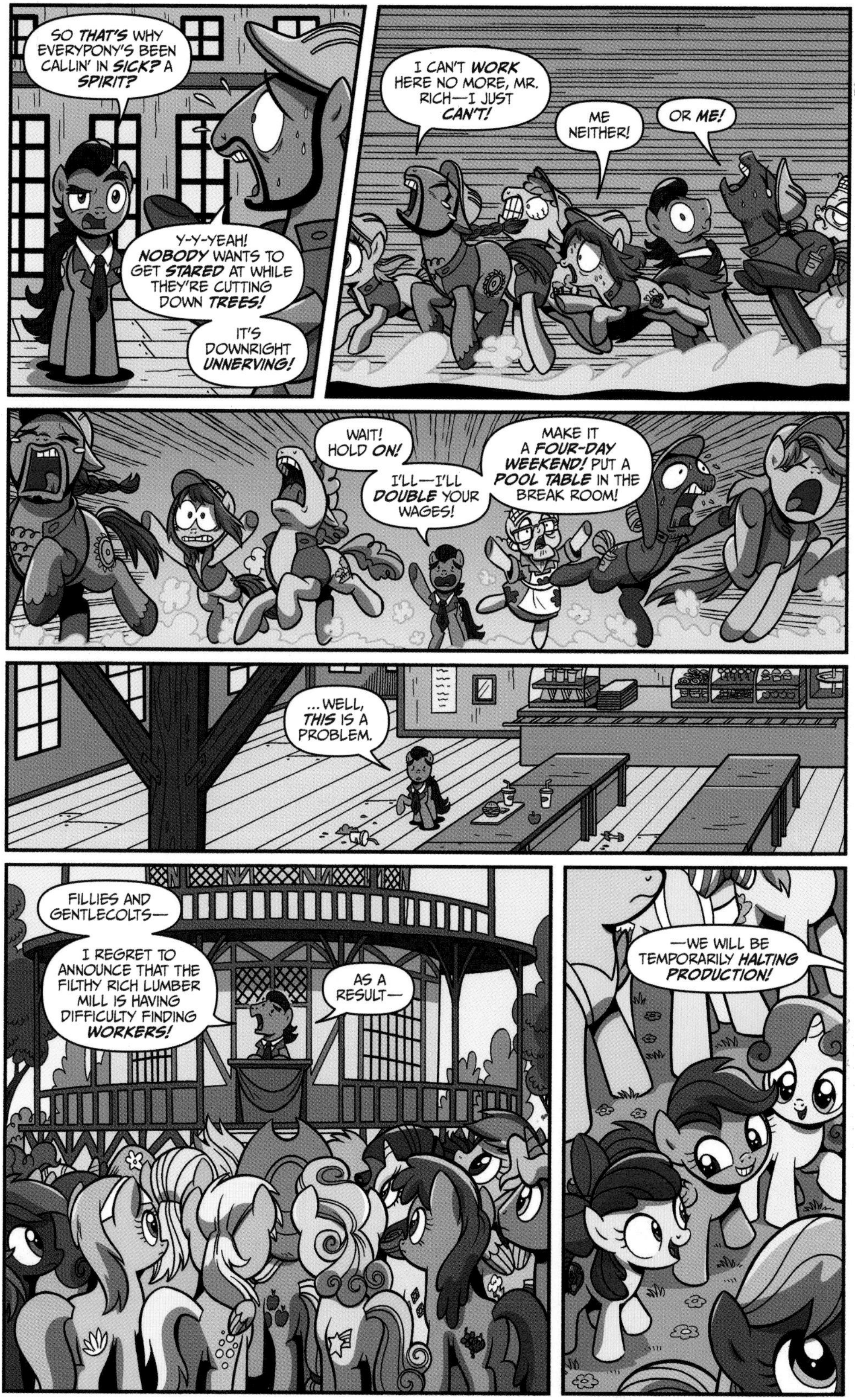
SO THAT'S WHY EVERYPONY'S BEEN CALLIN' IN SICK? A SPIRIT?
Y-Y-YEAH! NOBODY WANTS TO GET STARED AT WHILE THEY'RE CUTTING DOWN TREES!
IT'S DOWNRIGHT UNNERVING!
I CAN'T WORK HERE NO MORE, MR. RICH—I JUST CAN'T!
ME NEITHER!
OR ME!
WAIT! HOLD ON!
I'LL—I'LL DOUBLE YOUR WAGES!
MAKE IT A FOUR-DAY WEEKEND! PUT A POOL TABLE IN THE BREAK ROOM!
...WELL, THIS IS A PROBLEM.
FILLIES AND GENTLECOLTS—
I REGRET TO ANNOUNCE THAT THE FILTHY RICH LUMBER MILL IS HAVING DIFFICULTY FINDING WORKERS!
AS A RESULT—
—WE WILL BE TEMPORARILY HALTING PRODUCTION!

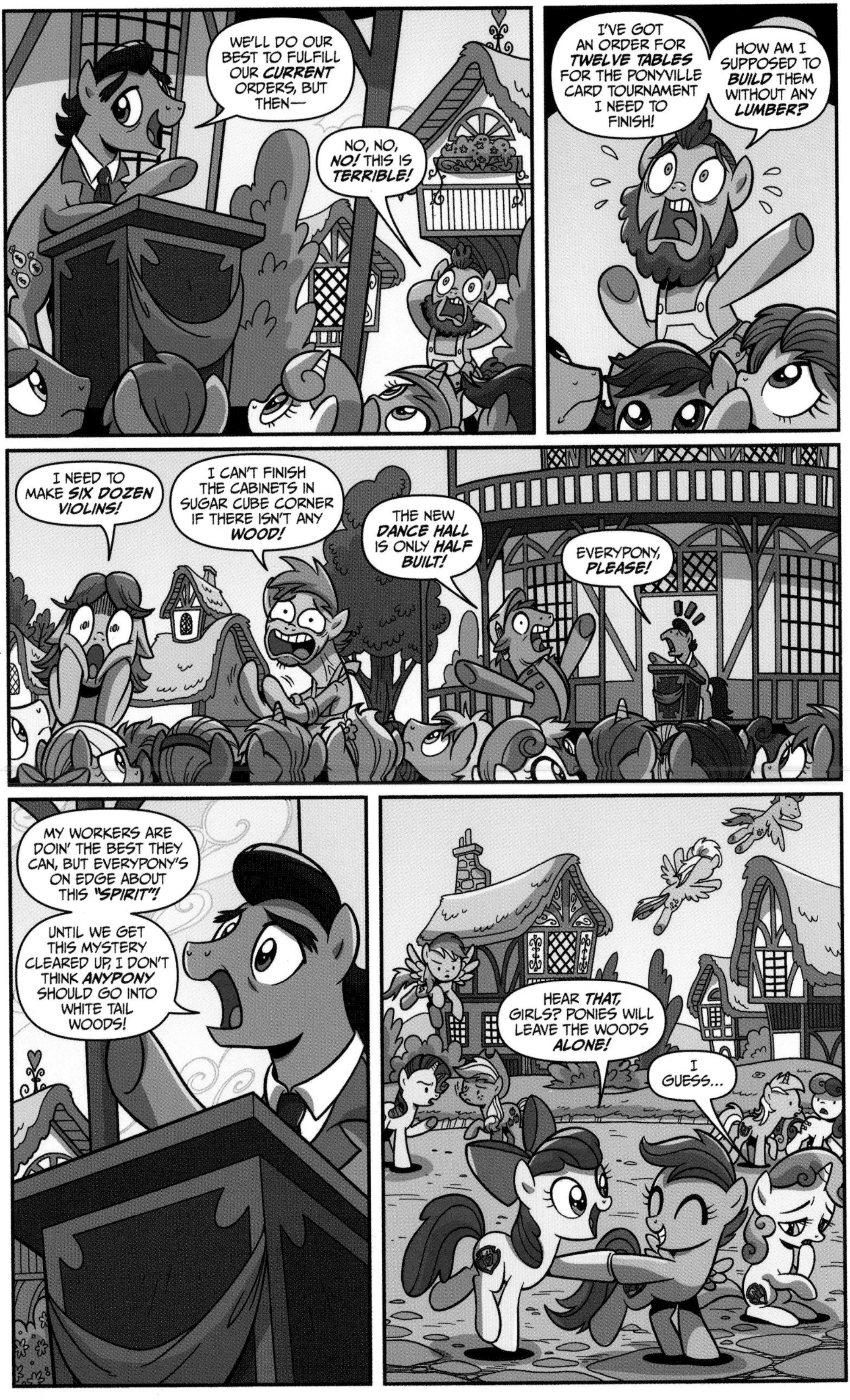
WE'LL DO OUR BEST TO FULFILL OUR *CURRENT* ORDERS, BUT THEN—
NO, NO, *NO!* THIS IS *TERRIBLE!*
I'VE GOT AN ORDER FOR *TWELVE TABLES* FOR THE PONYVILLE CARD TOURNAMENT I NEED TO FINISH!
HOW AM I SUPPOSED TO *BUILD* THEM WITHOUT ANY *LUMBER?*
I NEED TO MAKE *SIX DOZEN VIOLINS!*
I CAN'T FINISH THE CABINETS IN SUGAR CUBE CORNER IF THERE ISN'T ANY *WOOD!*
THE NEW *DANCE HALL* IS ONLY *HALF BUILT!*
EVERYPONY, *PLEASE!*
MY WORKERS ARE DOIN' THE BEST THEY CAN, BUT EVERYPONY'S ON EDGE ABOUT THIS *"SPIRIT"!*
UNTIL WE GET THIS MYSTERY CLEARED UP, I DON'T THINK *ANYPONY* SHOULD GO INTO WHITE TAIL WOODS!
HEAR *THAT,* GIRLS? PONIES WILL LEAVE THE WOODS *ALONE!*
I GUESS...

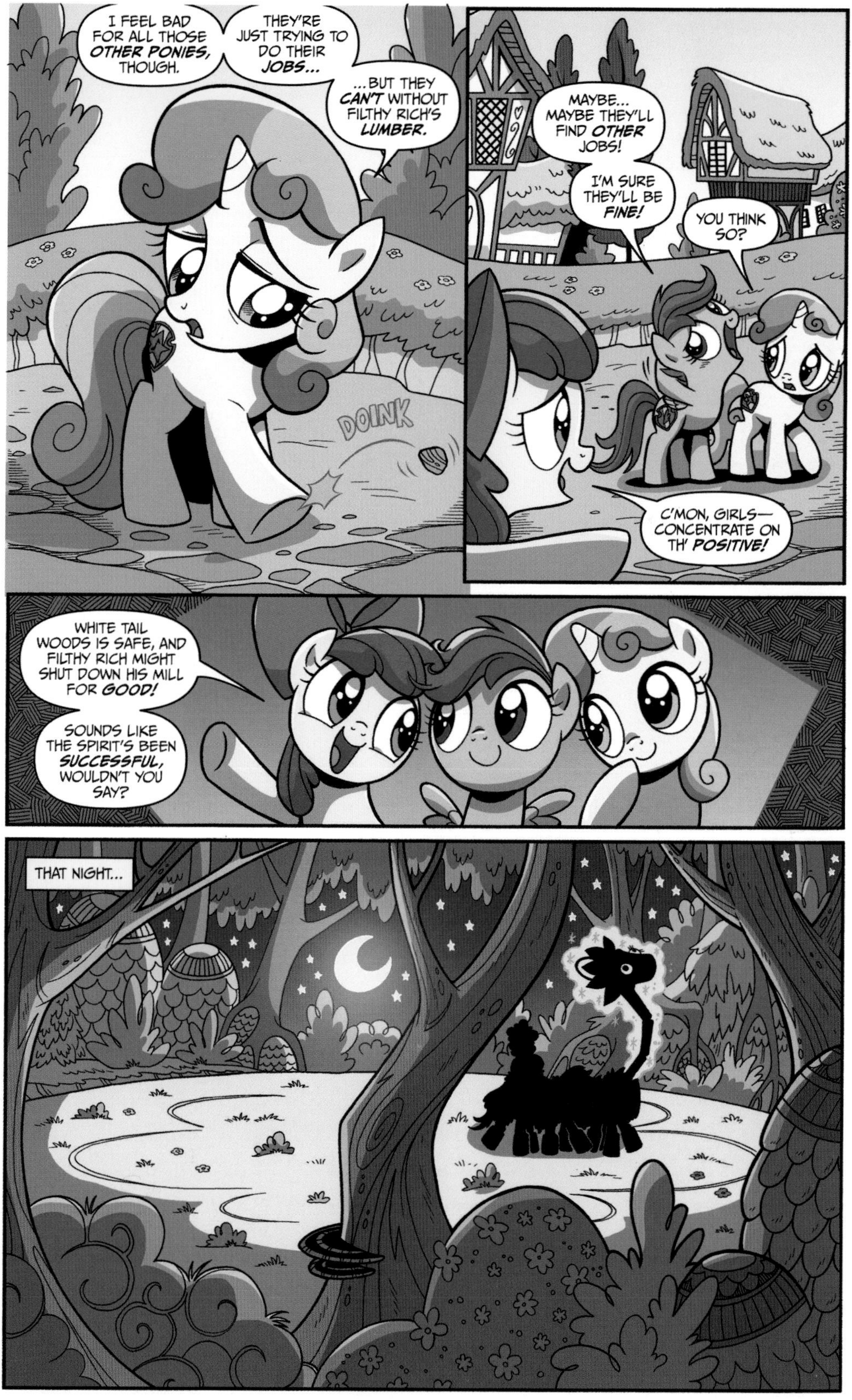

I FEEL BAD FOR ALL THOSE *OTHER PONIES,* THOUGH.
THEY'RE JUST TRYING TO DO THEIR *JOBS...*
...BUT THEY *CAN'T* WITHOUT FILTHY RICH'S *LUMBER.*
DOINK
MAYBE... MAYBE THEY'LL FIND *OTHER* JOBS!
I'M SURE THEY'LL BE *FINE!*
YOU THINK SO?
C'MON, GIRLS— CONCENTRATE ON TH' *POSITIVE!*
WHITE TAIL WOODS IS SAFE, AND FILTHY RICH MIGHT SHUT DOWN HIS MILL FOR *GOOD!*
SOUNDS LIKE THE SPIRIT'S BEEN *SUCCESSFUL,* WOULDN'T YOU SAY?
THAT NIGHT...

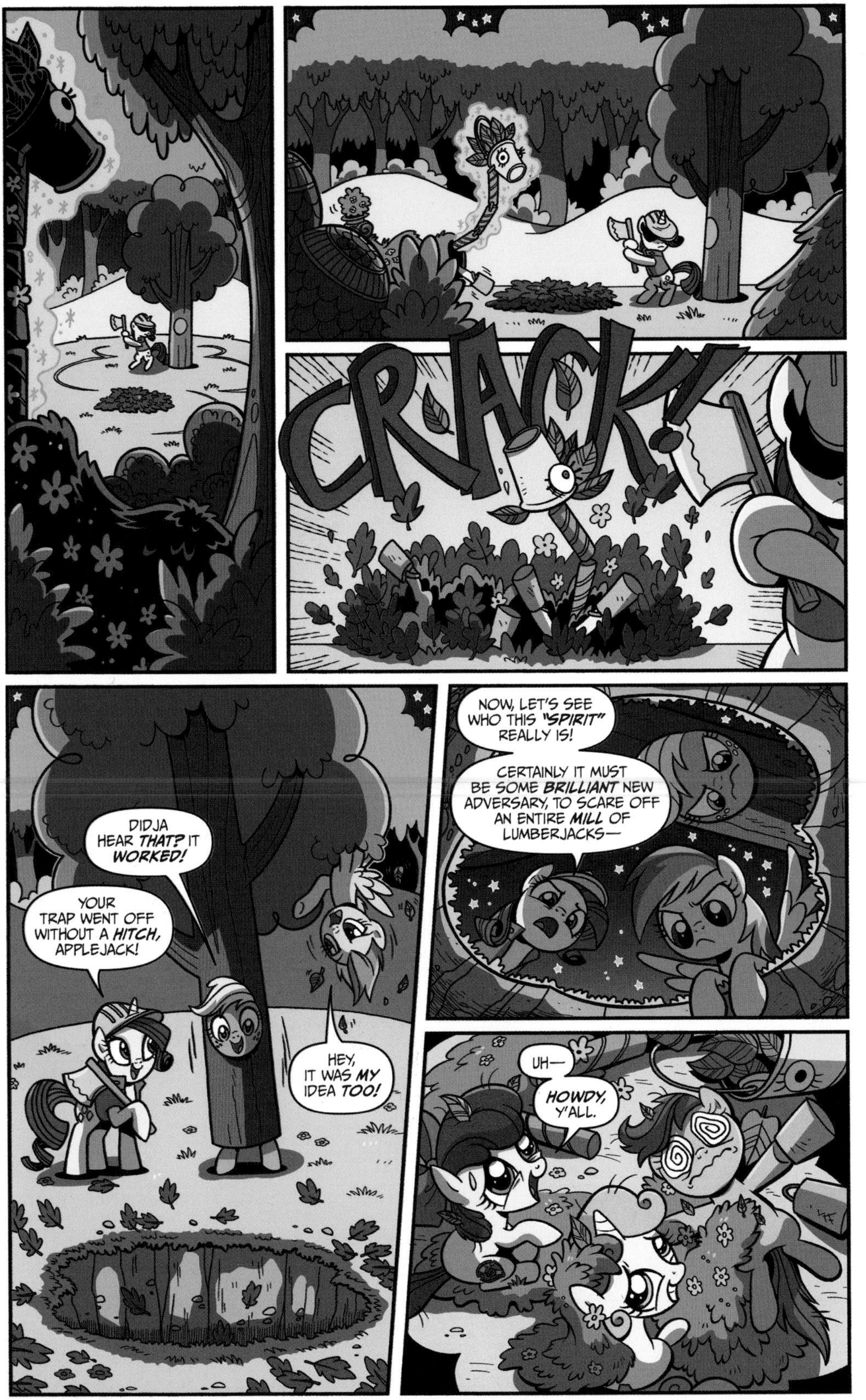
CRACK!!
NOW, LET'S SEE WHO THIS "SPIRIT" REALLY IS!
CERTAINLY IT MUST BE SOME BRILLIANT NEW ADVERSARY, TO SCARE OFF AN ENTIRE MILL OF LUMBERJACKS—
DIDJA HEAR THAT? IT WORKED!
YOUR TRAP WENT OFF WITHOUT A HITCH, APPLEJACK!
HEY, IT WAS MY IDEA TOO!
UH—
HOWDY, Y'ALL.

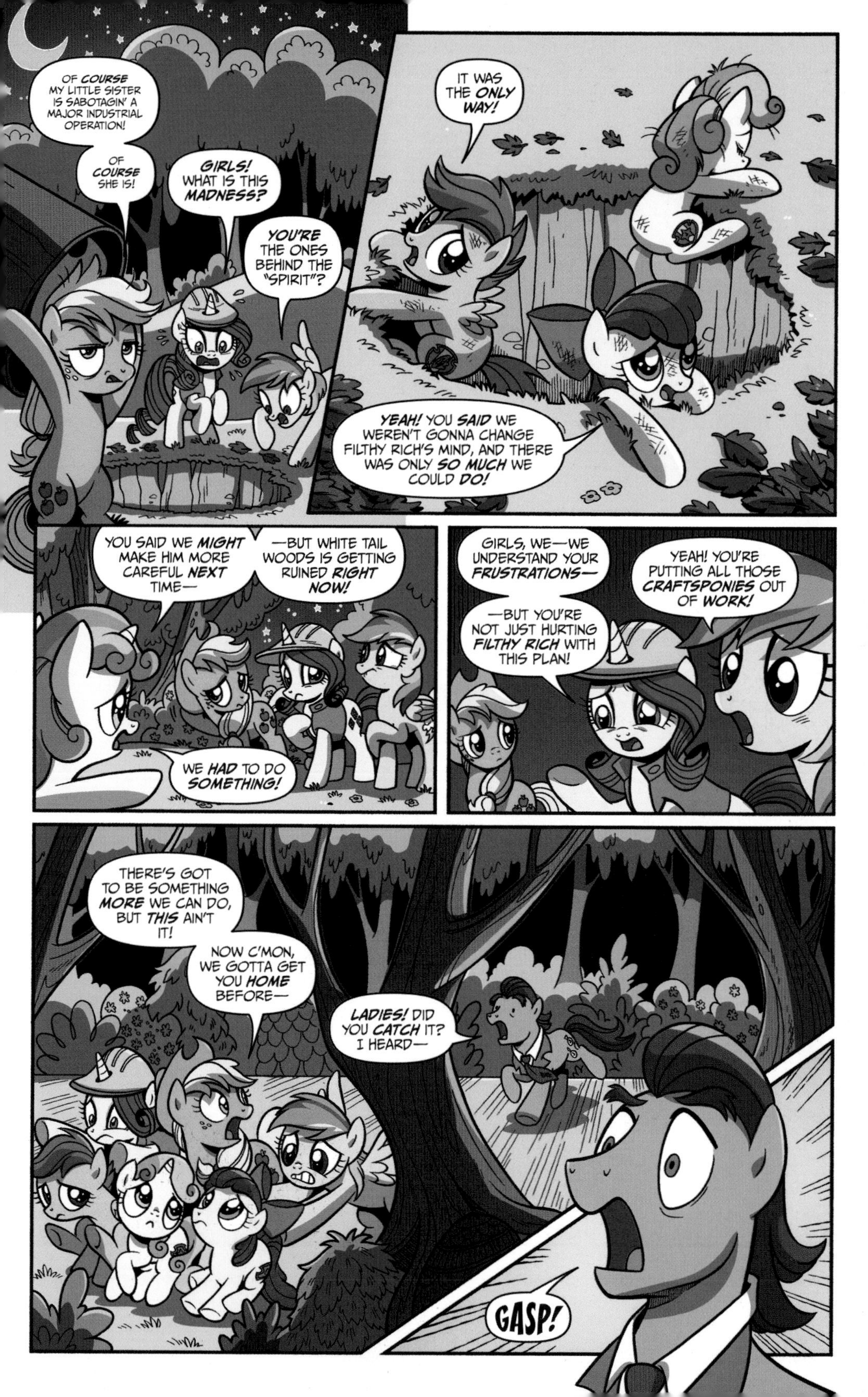

OF COURSE MY LITTLE SISTER IS SABOTAGIN' A MAJOR INDUSTRIAL OPERATION!
OF COURSE SHE IS!
GIRLS! WHAT IS THIS MADNESS?
YOU'RE THE ONES BEHIND THE "SPIRIT"?
IT WAS THE ONLY WAY!
YEAH! YOU SAID WE WEREN'T GONNA CHANGE FILTHY RICH'S MIND, AND THERE WAS ONLY SO MUCH WE COULD DO!
YOU SAID WE MIGHT MAKE HIM MORE CAREFUL NEXT TIME—
—BUT WHITE TAIL WOODS IS GETTING RUINED RIGHT NOW!
WE HAD TO DO SOMETHING!
GIRLS, WE—WE UNDERSTAND YOUR FRUSTRATIONS—
—BUT YOU'RE NOT JUST HURTING FILTHY RICH WITH THIS PLAN!
YEAH! YOU'RE PUTTING ALL THOSE CRAFTSPONIES OUT OF WORK!
THERE'S GOT TO BE SOMETHING MORE WE CAN DO, BUT THIS AIN'T IT!
NOW C'MON, WE GOTTA GET YOU HOME BEFORE—
LADIES! DID YOU CATCH IT? I HEARD—
GASP!

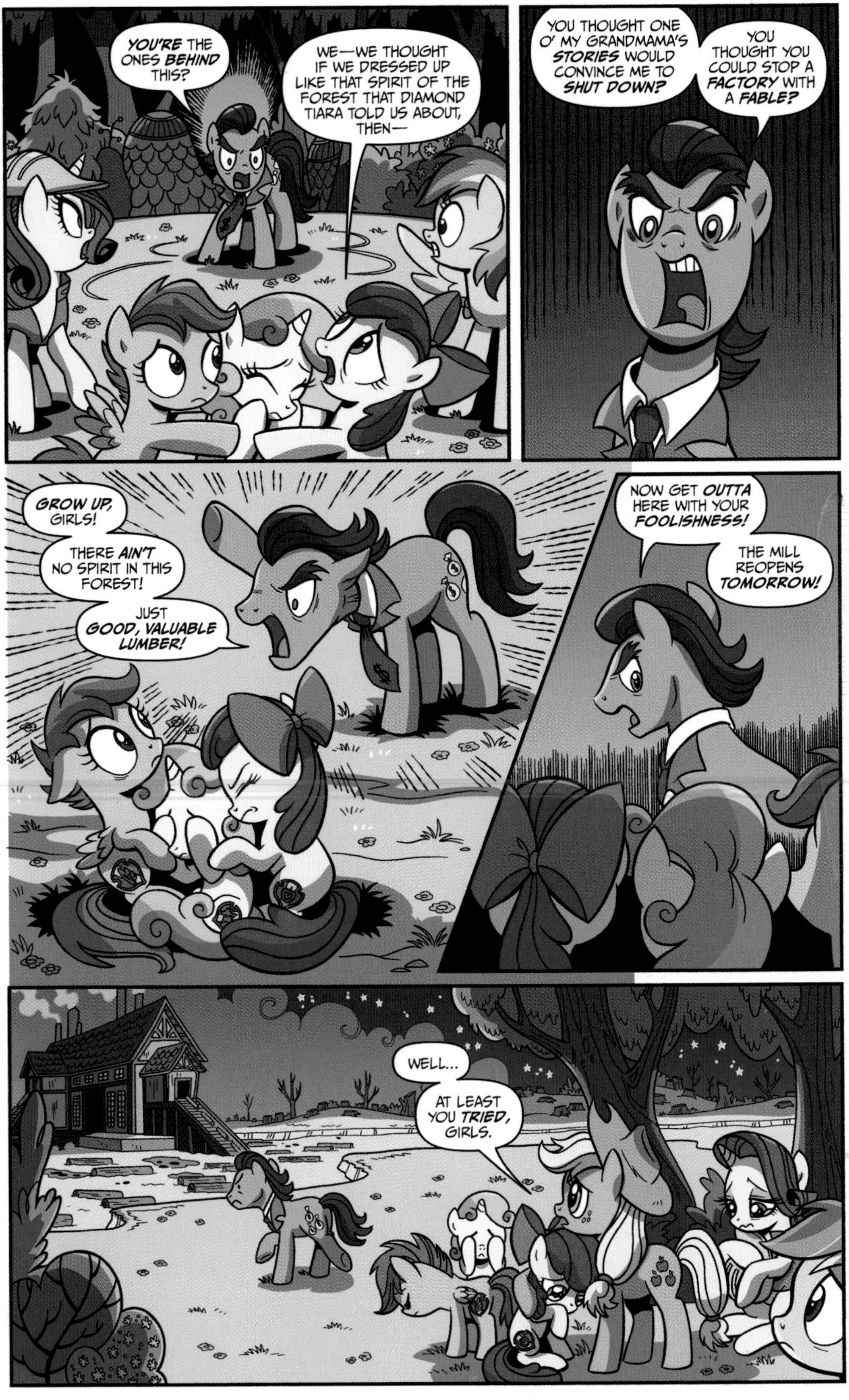
YOU'RE THE ONES BEHIND THIS?
WE—WE THOUGHT IF WE DRESSED UP LIKE THAT SPIRIT OF THE FOREST THAT DIAMOND TIARA TOLD US ABOUT, THEN—
YOU THOUGHT ONE O' MY GRANDMAMA'S STORIES WOULD CONVINCE ME TO SHUT DOWN?
YOU THOUGHT YOU COULD STOP A FACTORY WITH A FABLE?
GROW UP, GIRLS!
THERE AIN'T NO SPIRIT IN THIS FOREST!
JUST GOOD, VALUABLE LUMBER!
NOW GET OUTTA HERE WITH YOUR FOOLISHNESS!
THE MILL REOPENS TOMORROW!
WELL...
AT LEAST YOU TRIED, GIRLS.

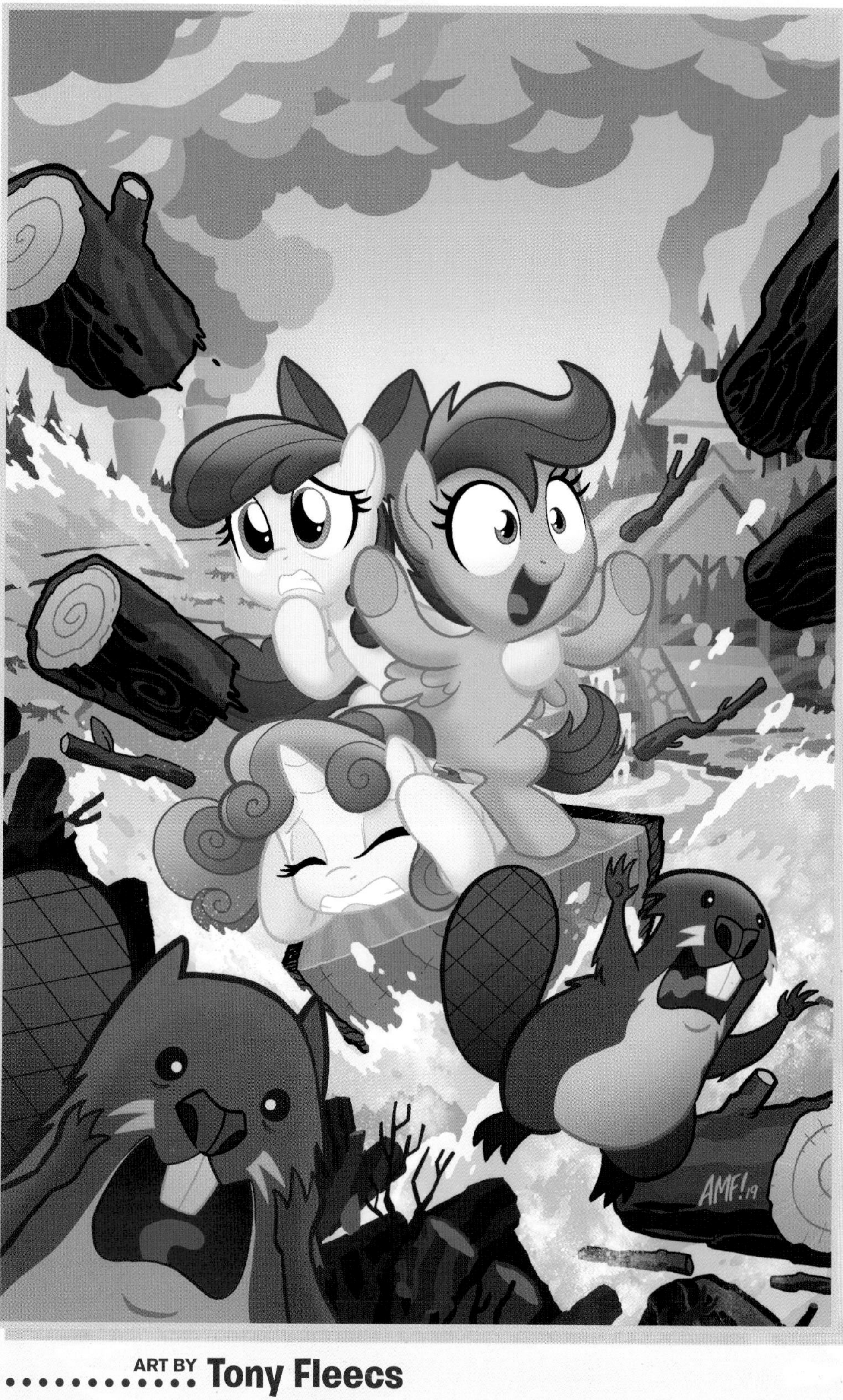
AMF! 19

ART BY **Tony Fleecs**

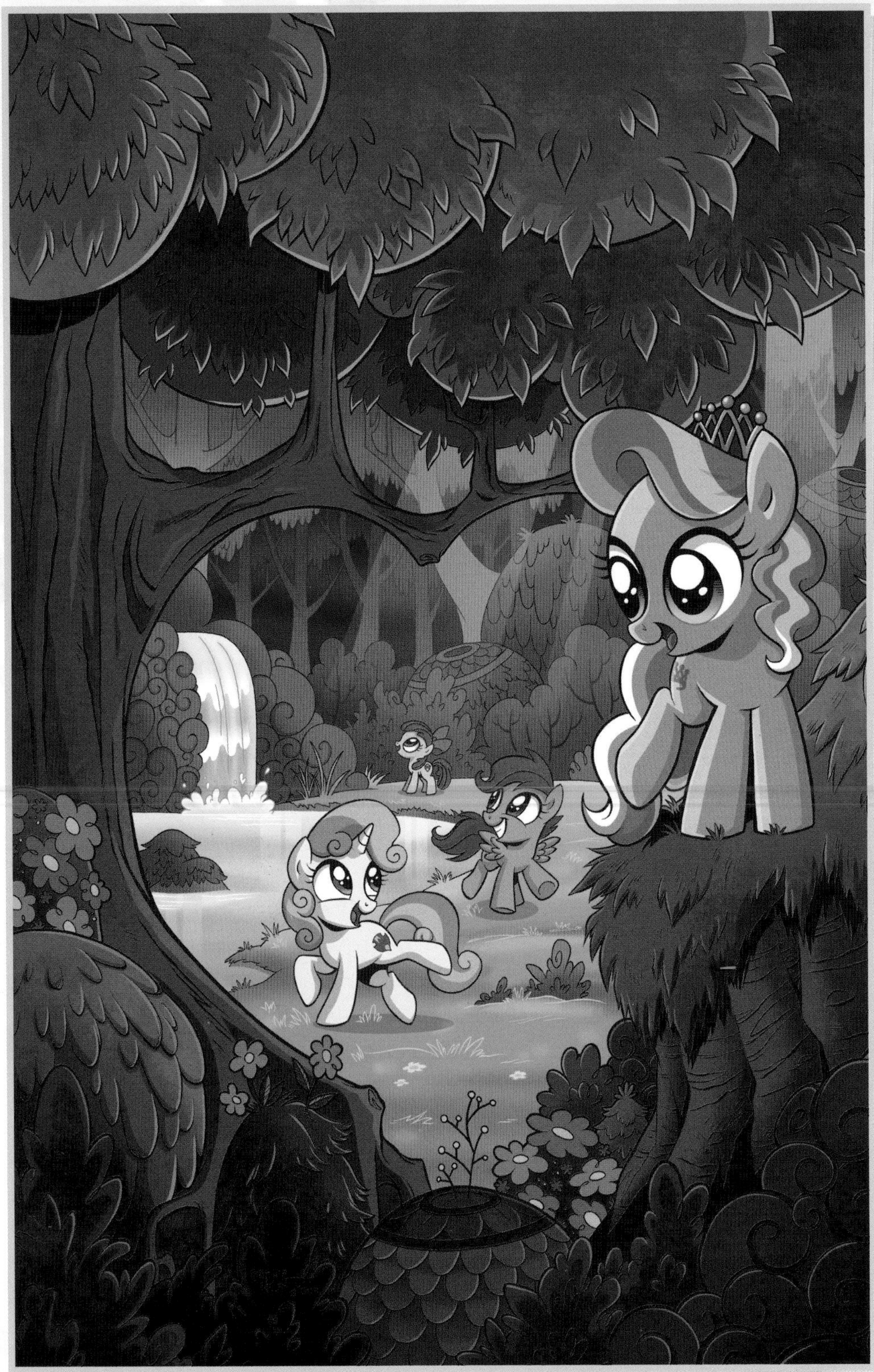

ART BY **Brenda Hickey**

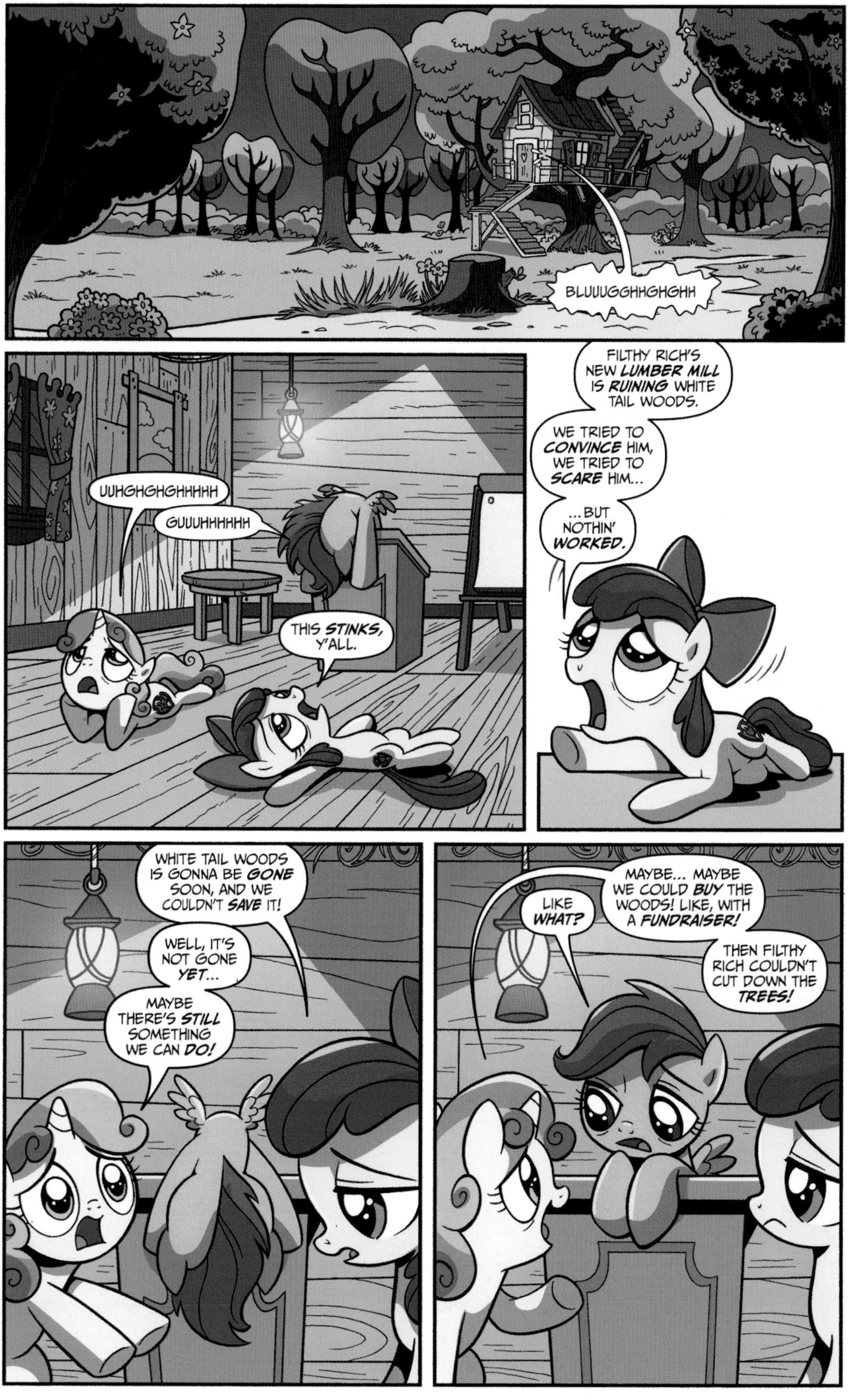
BLUUUGGHHGHGHH
UUHGHGHGHHHHH
GUUUHHHHHH
THIS STINKS, Y'ALL.
FILTHY RICH'S NEW LUMBER MILL IS RUINING WHITE TAIL WOODS.
WE TRIED TO CONVINCE HIM, WE TRIED TO SCARE HIM...
...BUT NOTHIN' WORKED.
WHITE TAIL WOODS IS GONNA BE GONE SOON, AND WE COULDN'T SAVE IT!
WELL, IT'S NOT GONE YET...
MAYBE THERE'S STILL SOMETHING WE CAN DO!
LIKE WHAT?
MAYBE... MAYBE WE COULD BUY THE WOODS! LIKE, WITH A FUNDRAISER!
THEN FILTHY RICH COULDN'T CUT DOWN THE TREES!

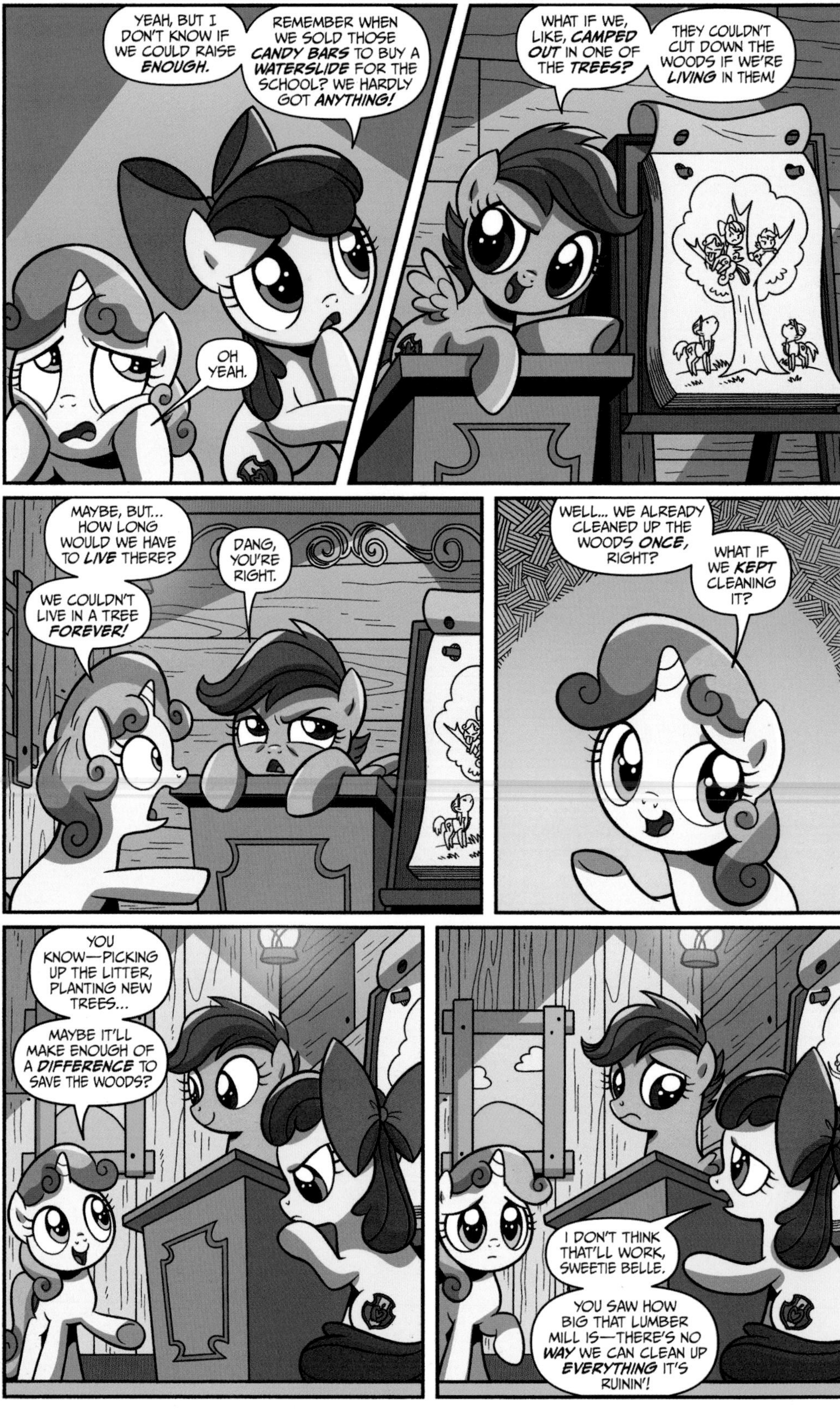
YEAH, BUT I DON'T KNOW IF WE COULD RAISE ENOUGH.
REMEMBER WHEN WE SOLD THOSE CANDY BARS TO BUY A WATERSLIDE FOR THE SCHOOL? WE HARDLY GOT ANYTHING!
OH YEAH.
WHAT IF WE, LIKE, CAMPED OUT IN ONE OF THE TREES?
THEY COULDN'T CUT DOWN THE WOODS IF WE'RE LIVING IN THEM!
MAYBE, BUT... HOW LONG WOULD WE HAVE TO LIVE THERE?
WE COULDN'T LIVE IN A TREE FOREVER!
DANG, YOU'RE RIGHT.
WELL... WE ALREADY CLEANED UP THE WOODS ONCE, RIGHT?
WHAT IF WE KEPT CLEANING IT?
YOU KNOW—PICKING UP THE LITTER, PLANTING NEW TREES...
MAYBE IT'LL MAKE ENOUGH OF A DIFFERENCE TO SAVE THE WOODS?
I DON'T THINK THAT'LL WORK, SWEETIE BELLE.
YOU SAW HOW BIG THAT LUMBER MILL IS—THERE'S NO WAY WE CAN CLEAN UP EVERYTHING IT'S RUININ'!

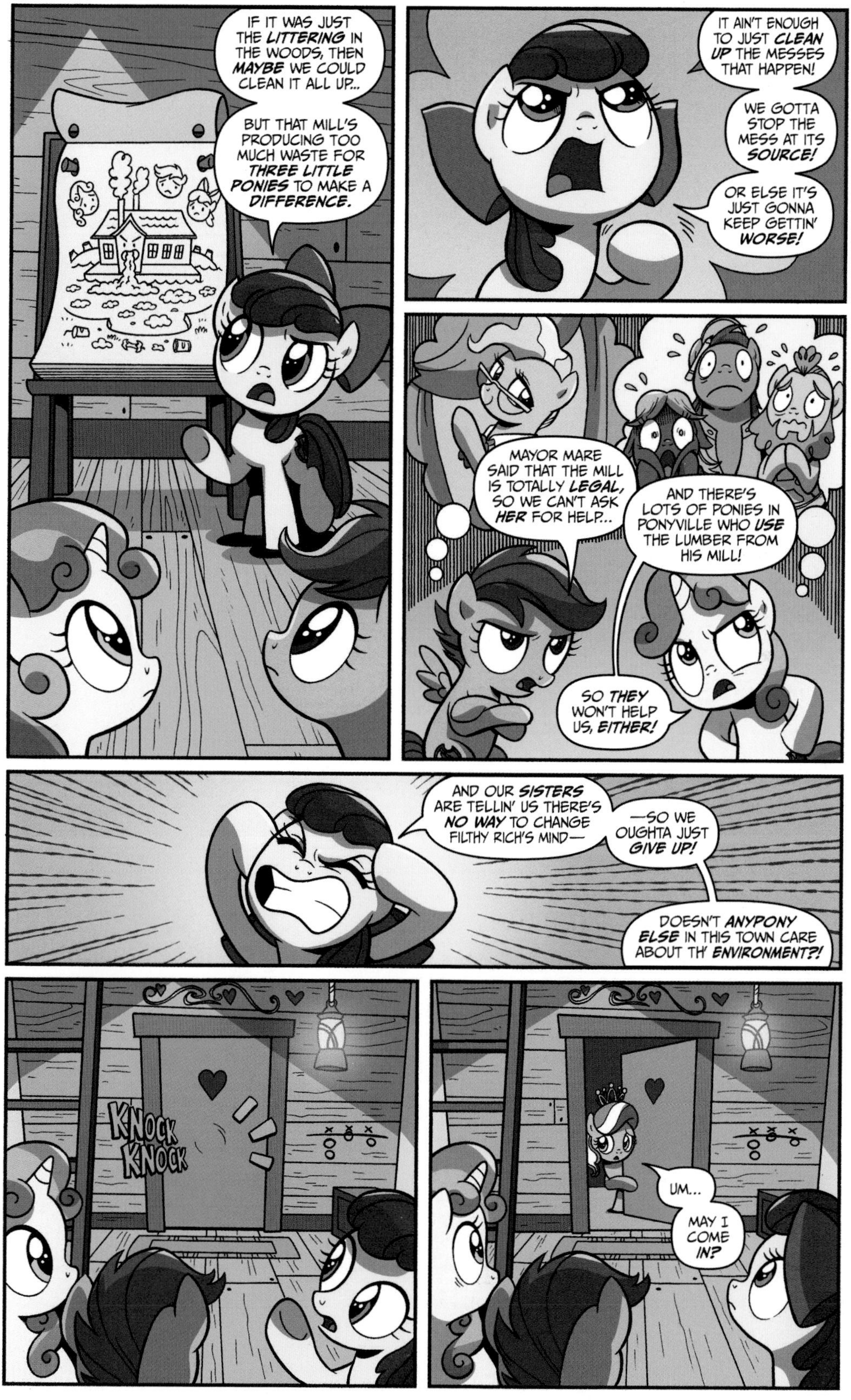
IF IT WAS JUST THE LITTERING IN THE WOODS, THEN MAYBE WE COULD CLEAN IT ALL UP...
BUT THAT MILL'S PRODUCING TOO MUCH WASTE FOR THREE LITTLE PONIES TO MAKE A DIFFERENCE.
IT AIN'T ENOUGH TO JUST CLEAN UP THE MESSES THAT HAPPEN!
WE GOTTA STOP THE MESS AT ITS SOURCE!
OR ELSE IT'S JUST GONNA KEEP GETTIN' WORSE!
MAYOR MARE SAID THAT THE MILL IS TOTALLY LEGAL, SO WE CAN'T ASK HER FOR HELP...
AND THERE'S LOTS OF PONIES IN PONYVILLE WHO USE THE LUMBER FROM HIS MILL!
SO THEY WON'T HELP US, EITHER!
AND OUR SISTERS ARE TELLIN' US THERE'S NO WAY TO CHANGE FILTHY RICH'S MIND—
—SO WE OUGHTA JUST GIVE UP!
DOESN'T ANYPONY ELSE IN THIS TOWN CARE ABOUT TH' ENVIRONMENT?!
KNOCK KNOCK
UM...
MAY I COME IN?

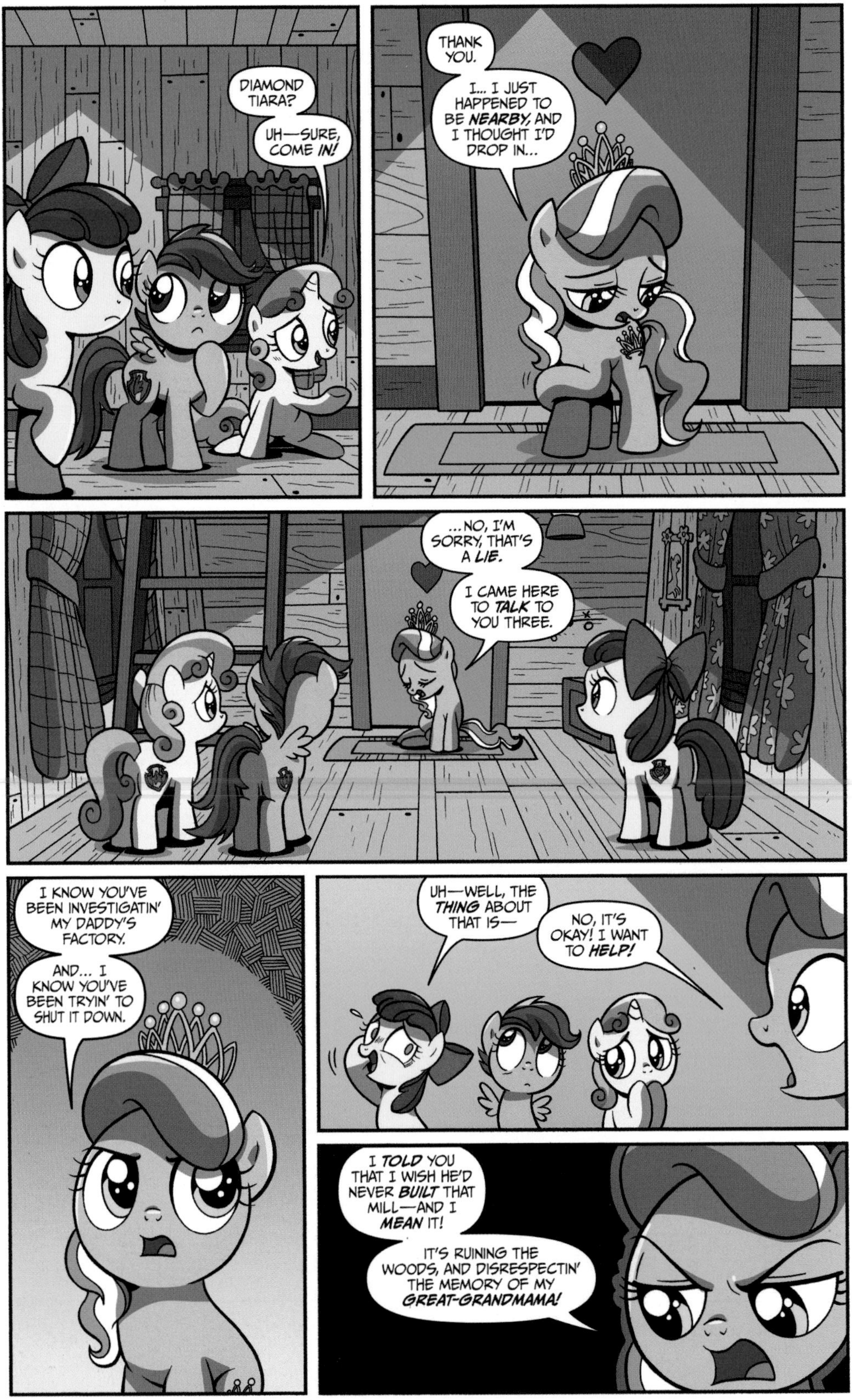
DIAMOND TIARA?
UH—SURE, COME IN!
THANK YOU.
I... I JUST HAPPENED TO BE NEARBY, AND I THOUGHT I'D DROP IN...
...NO, I'M SORRY, THAT'S A LIE.
I CAME HERE TO TALK TO YOU THREE.
I KNOW YOU'VE BEEN INVESTIGATIN' MY DADDY'S FACTORY.
AND... I KNOW YOU'VE BEEN TRYIN' TO SHUT IT DOWN.
UH—WELL, THE THING ABOUT THAT IS—
NO, IT'S OKAY! I WANT TO HELP!
I TOLD YOU THAT I WISH HE'D NEVER BUILT THAT MILL—AND I MEAN IT!
IT'S RUINING THE WOODS, AND DISRESPECTIN' THE MEMORY OF MY GREAT-GRANDMAMA!

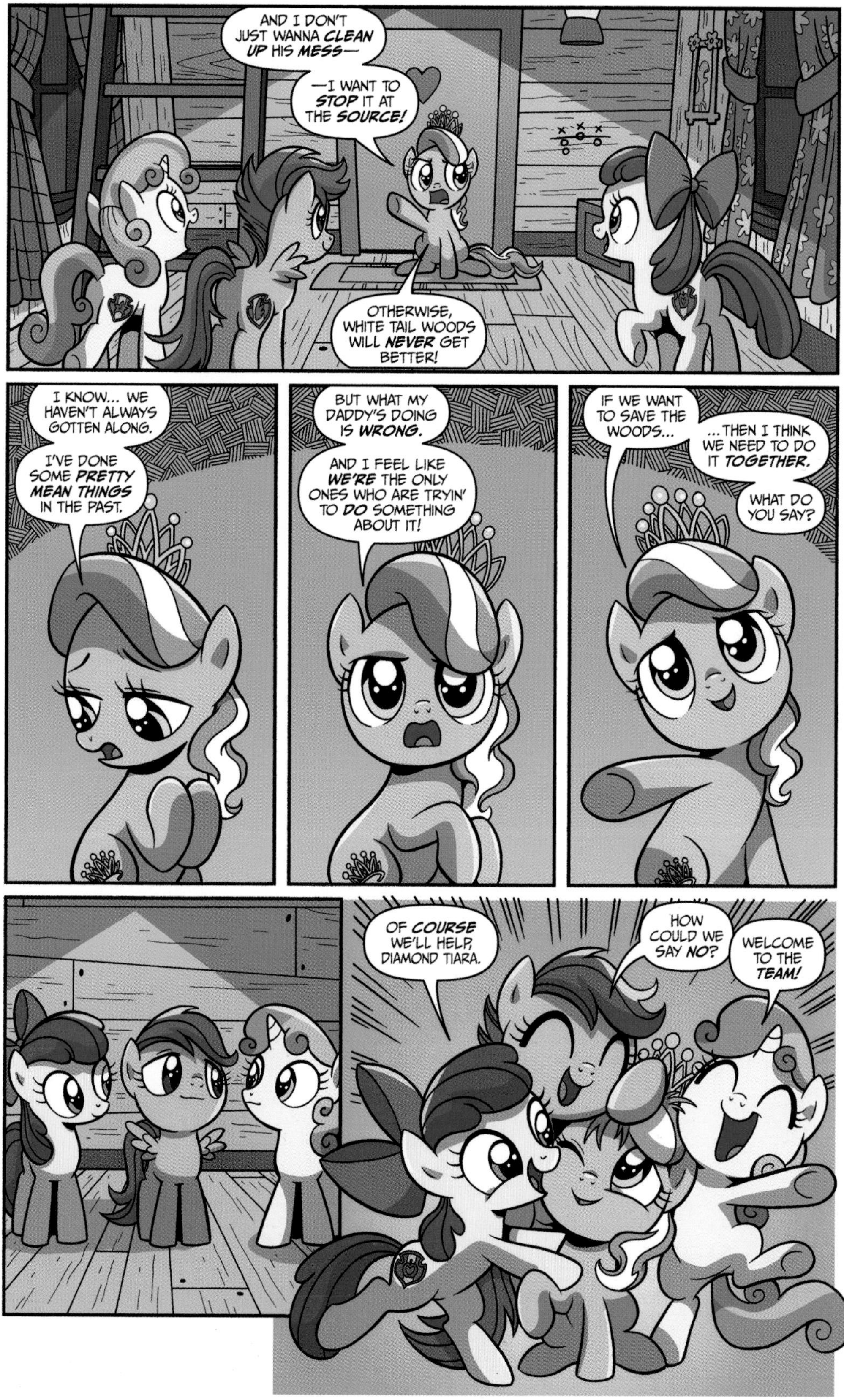

AND I DON'T JUST WANNA CLEAN UP HIS MESS—
—I WANT TO STOP IT AT THE SOURCE!
OTHERWISE, WHITE TAIL WOODS WILL NEVER GET BETTER!
I KNOW... WE HAVEN'T ALWAYS GOTTEN ALONG.
I'VE DONE SOME PRETTY MEAN THINGS IN THE PAST.
BUT WHAT MY DADDY'S DOING IS WRONG.
AND I FEEL LIKE WE'RE THE ONLY ONES WHO ARE TRYIN' TO DO SOMETHING ABOUT IT!
IF WE WANT TO SAVE THE WOODS...
...THEN I THINK WE NEED TO DO IT TOGETHER.
WHAT DO YOU SAY?
OF COURSE WE'LL HELP, DIAMOND TIARA.
HOW COULD WE SAY NO?
WELCOME TO THE TEAM!

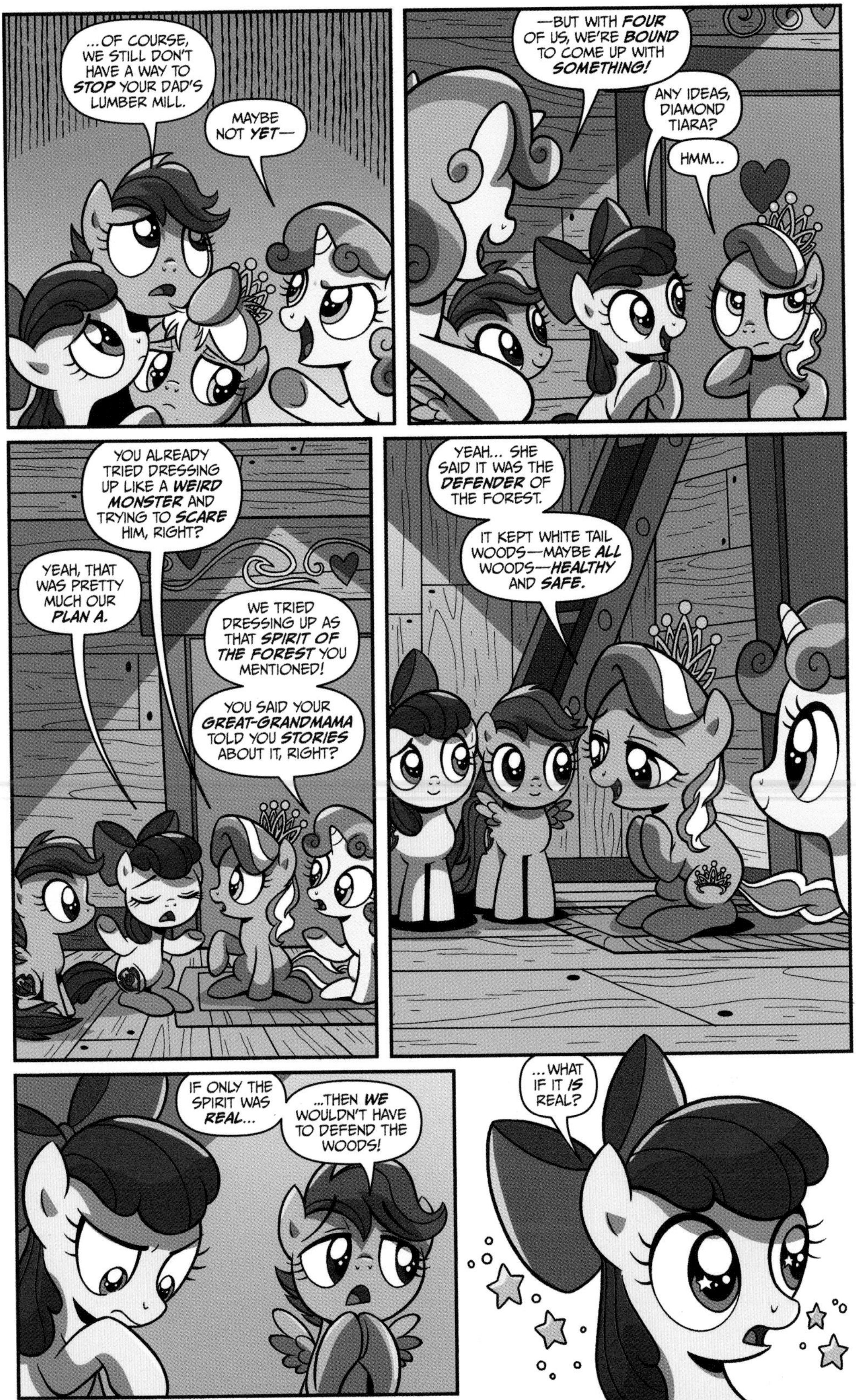
...OF COURSE, WE STILL DON'T HAVE A WAY TO STOP YOUR DAD'S LUMBER MILL.
MAYBE NOT YET—
—BUT WITH FOUR OF US, WE'RE BOUND TO COME UP WITH SOMETHING!
ANY IDEAS, DIAMOND TIARA?
HMM...
YOU ALREADY TRIED DRESSING UP LIKE A WEIRD MONSTER AND TRYING TO SCARE HIM, RIGHT?
YEAH, THAT WAS PRETTY MUCH OUR PLAN A.
WE TRIED DRESSING UP AS THAT SPIRIT OF THE FOREST YOU MENTIONED!
YOU SAID YOUR GREAT-GRANDMAMA TOLD YOU STORIES ABOUT IT, RIGHT?
YEAH... SHE SAID IT WAS THE DEFENDER OF THE FOREST.
IT KEPT WHITE TAIL WOODS—MAYBE ALL WOODS—HEALTHY AND SAFE.
IF ONLY THE SPIRIT WAS REAL...
...THEN WE WOULDN'T HAVE TO DEFEND THE WOODS!
...WHAT IF IT IS REAL?

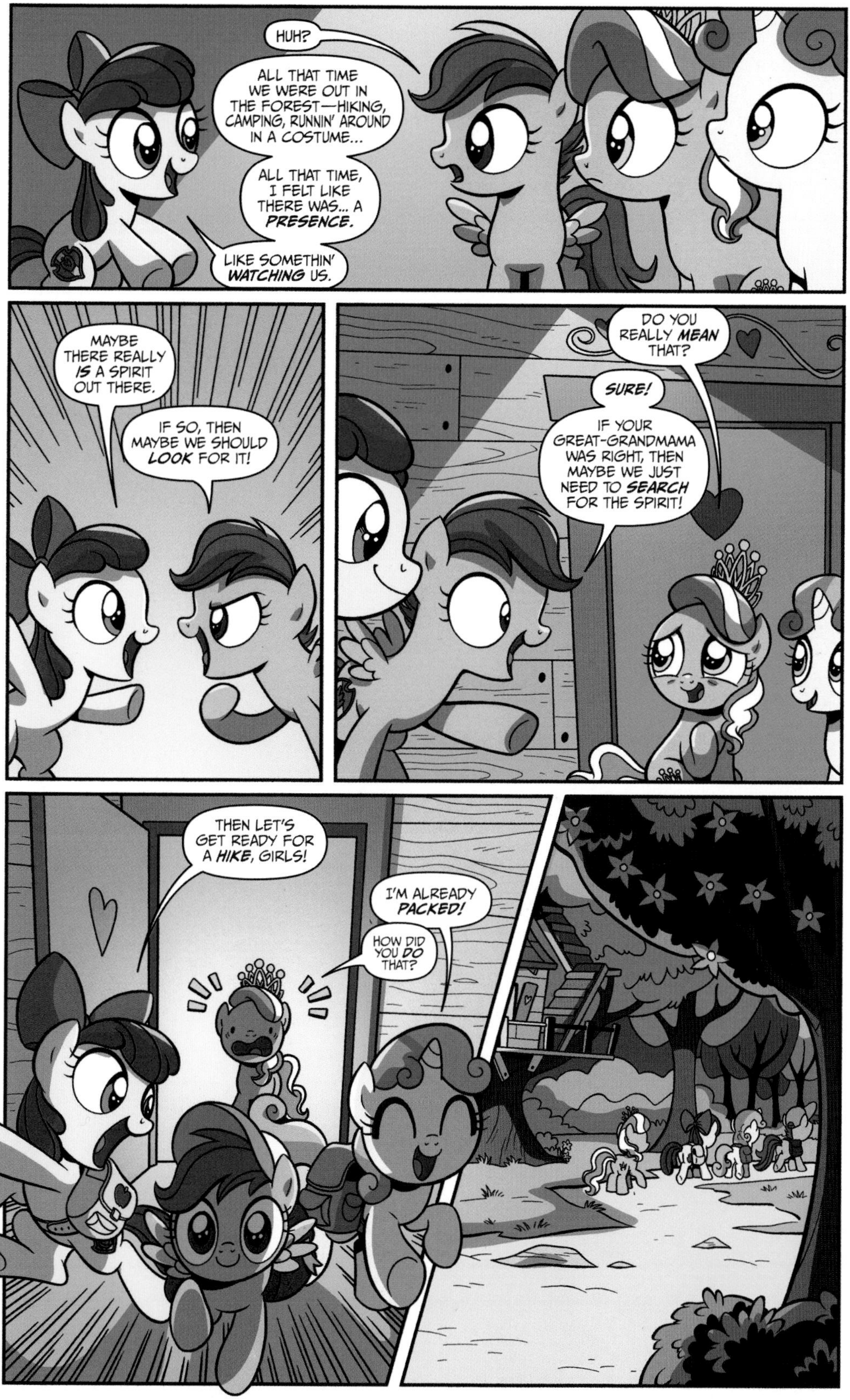
HUH?
ALL THAT TIME WE WERE OUT IN THE FOREST—HIKING, CAMPING, RUNNIN' AROUND IN A COSTUME...
ALL THAT TIME, I FELT LIKE THERE WAS... A PRESENCE.
LIKE SOMETHIN' WATCHING US.
MAYBE THERE REALLY IS A SPIRIT OUT THERE.
IF SO, THEN MAYBE WE SHOULD LOOK FOR IT!
DO YOU REALLY MEAN THAT?
SURE!
IF YOUR GREAT-GRANDMAMA WAS RIGHT, THEN MAYBE WE JUST NEED TO SEARCH FOR THE SPIRIT!
THEN LET'S GET READY FOR A HIKE, GIRLS!
I'M ALREADY PACKED!
HOW DID YOU DO THAT?

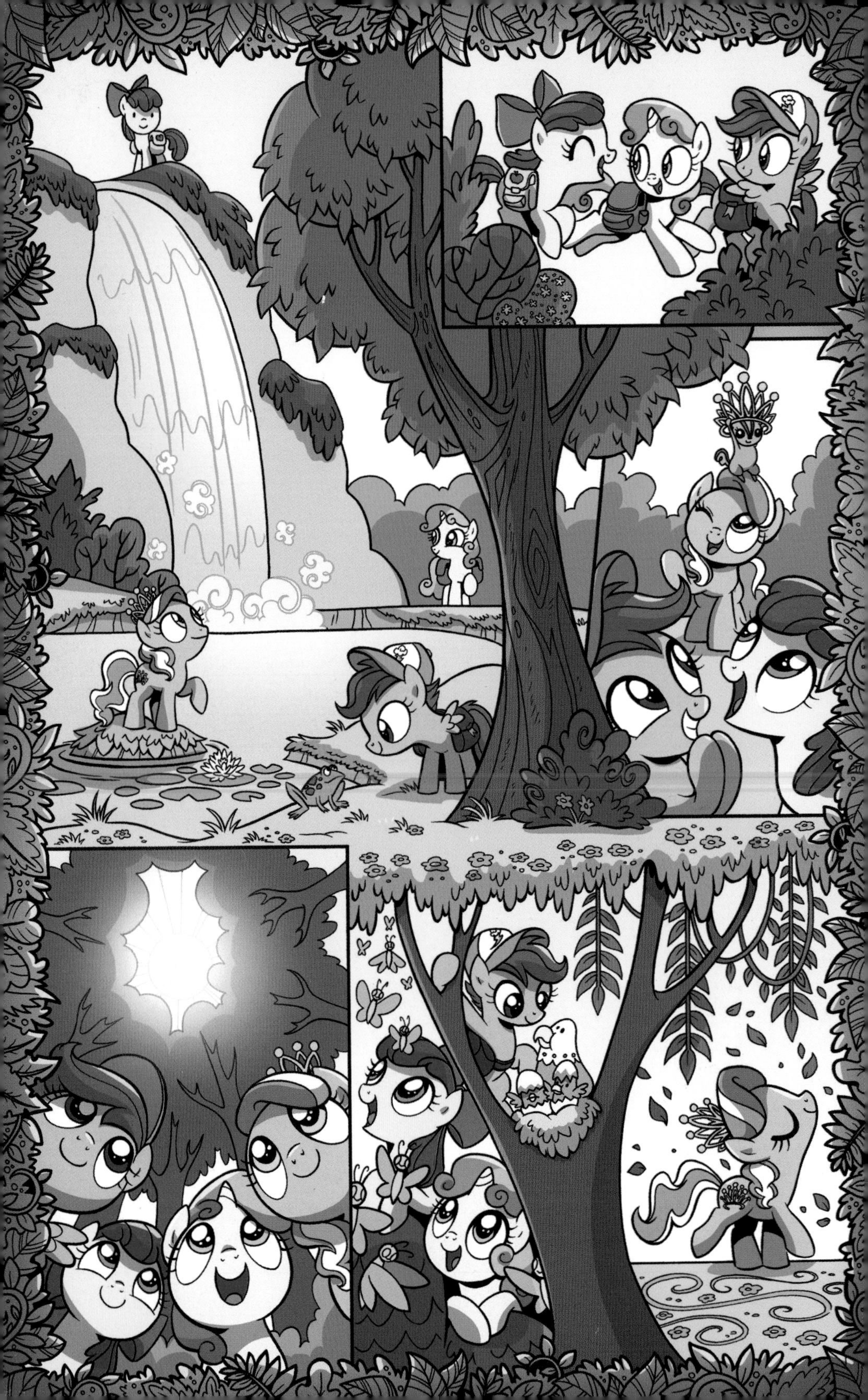

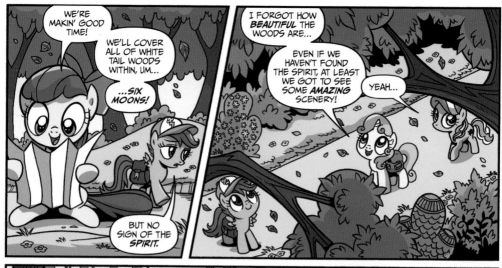

WE'RE MAKIN' GOOD TIME!

WE'LL COVER ALL OF WHITE TAIL WOODS WITHIN, UM...

...SIX MOONS!

BUT NO SIGN OF THE SPIRIT.

I FORGOT HOW *BEAUTIFUL* THE WOODS ARE...

EVEN IF WE HAVEN'T FOUND THE SPIRIT, AT LEAST WE GOT TO SEE SOME *AMAZING* SCENERY!

YEAH...

I'VE BEEN SO WORRIED ABOUT EVERYTHING...

...I FORGOT WHAT WE WERE TRYING TO *PROTECT.*

THIS PLACE IS *BEAUTIFUL.*

I THINK THERE'S SOMEPONY *ELSE* WHO SHOULD SEE IT.

HUH?

DO YOU WANT US TO COME WITH YOU, DIAMOND?

THANKS, GIRLS... BUT THIS IS SOMEPONY I SHOULD SEE *ALONE.*

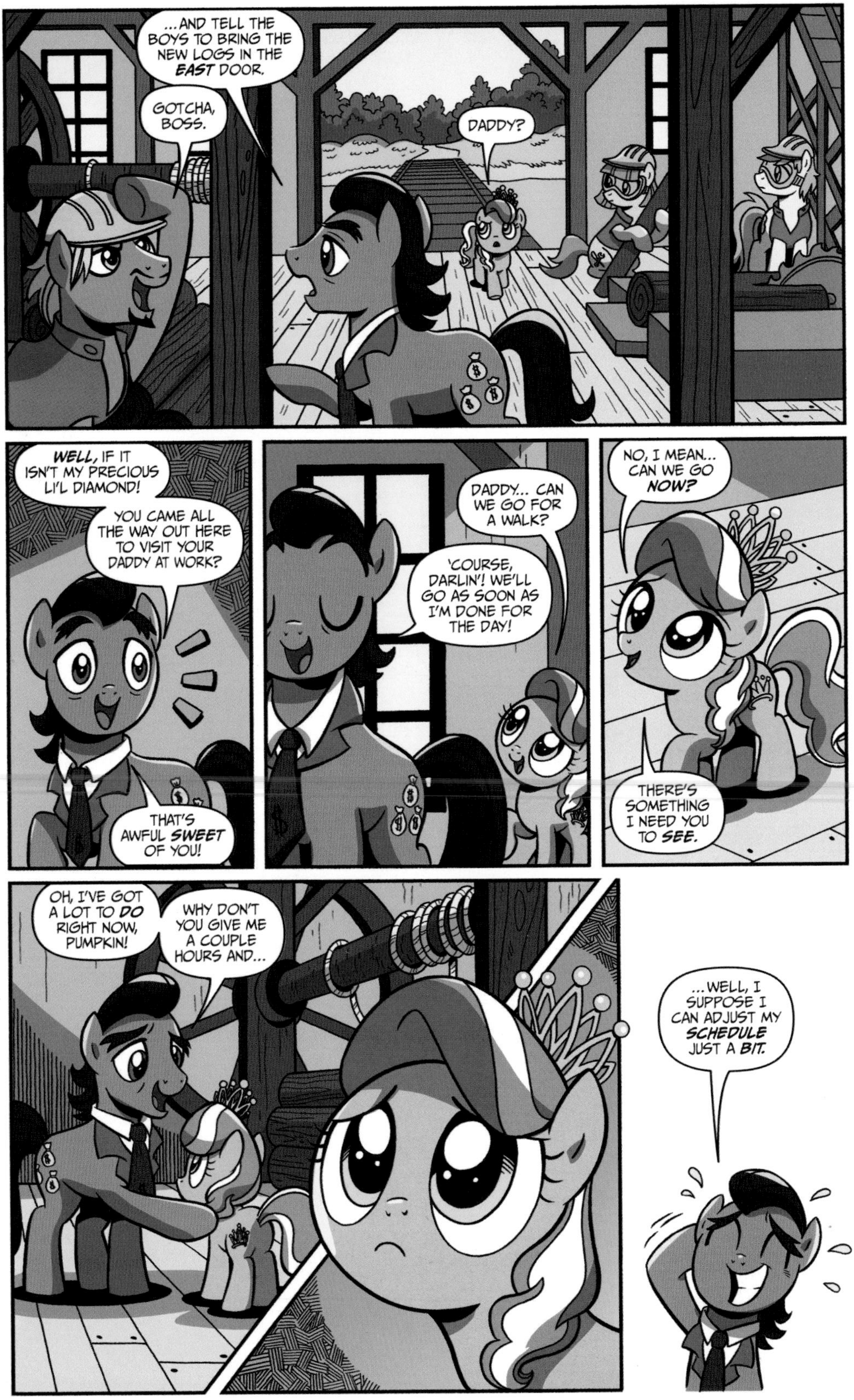
...AND TELL THE BOYS TO BRING THE NEW LOGS IN THE EAST DOOR.
GOTCHA, BOSS.
DADDY?
WELL, IF IT ISN'T MY PRECIOUS LI'L DIAMOND!
YOU CAME ALL THE WAY OUT HERE TO VISIT YOUR DADDY AT WORK?
THAT'S AWFUL SWEET OF YOU!
DADDY... CAN WE GO FOR A WALK?
'COURSE, DARLIN'! WE'LL GO AS SOON AS I'M DONE FOR THE DAY!
NO, I MEAN... CAN WE GO NOW?
THERE'S SOMETHING I NEED YOU TO SEE.
OH, I'VE GOT A LOT TO DO RIGHT NOW, PUMPKIN!
WHY DON'T YOU GIVE ME A COUPLE HOURS AND...
...WELL, I SUPPOSE I CAN ADJUST MY SCHEDULE JUST A BIT.

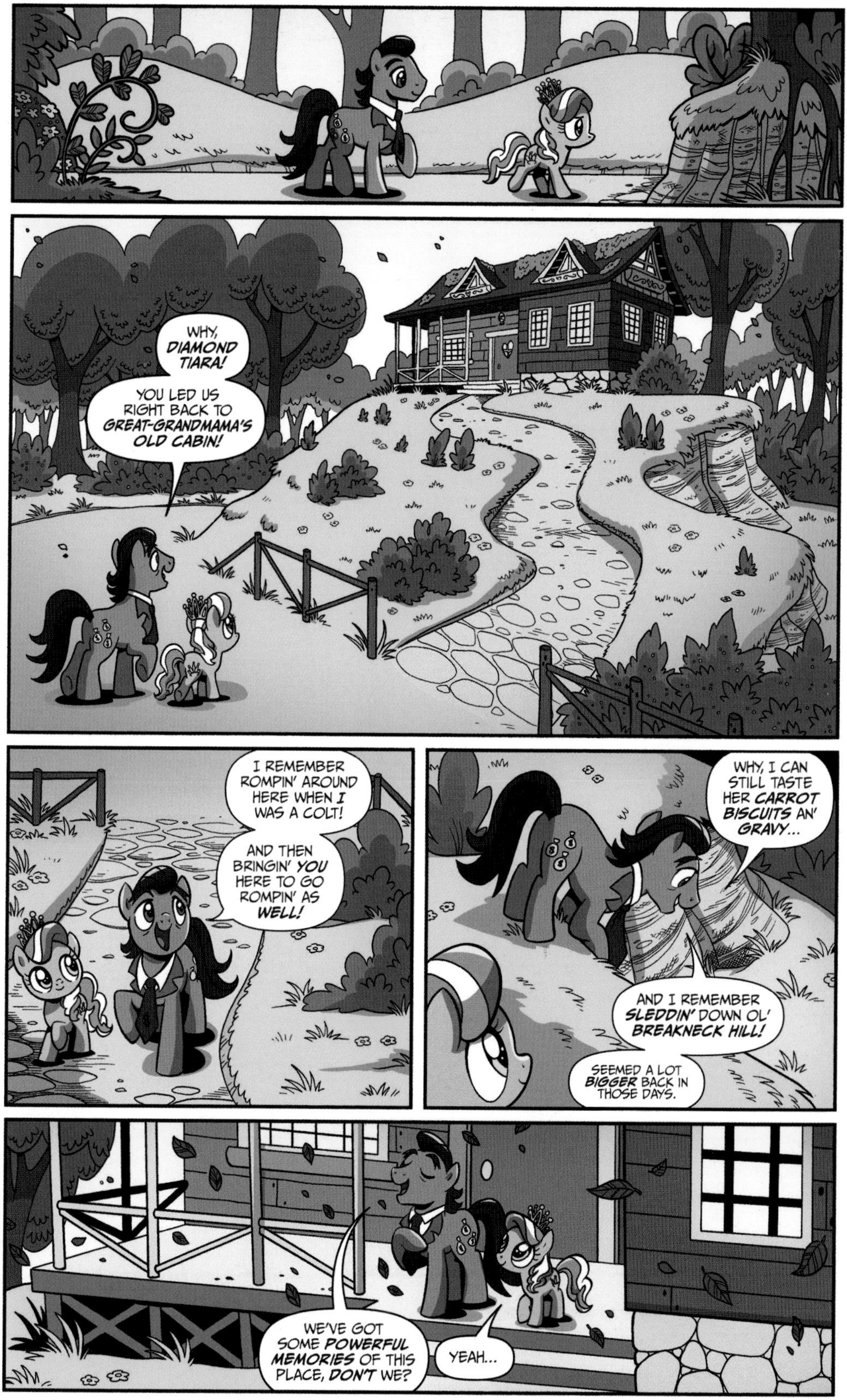
WHY, DIAMOND TIARA!
YOU LED US RIGHT BACK TO GREAT-GRANDMAMA'S OLD CABIN!
I REMEMBER ROMPIN' AROUND HERE WHEN I WAS A COLT!
AND THEN BRINGIN' YOU HERE TO GO ROMPIN' AS WELL!
WHY, I CAN STILL TASTE HER CARROT BISCUITS AN' GRAVY...
AND I REMEMBER SLEDDIN' DOWN OL' BREAKNECK HILL!
SEEMED A LOT BIGGER BACK IN THOSE DAYS.
WE'VE GOT SOME POWERFUL MEMORIES OF THIS PLACE, DON'T WE?
YEAH...

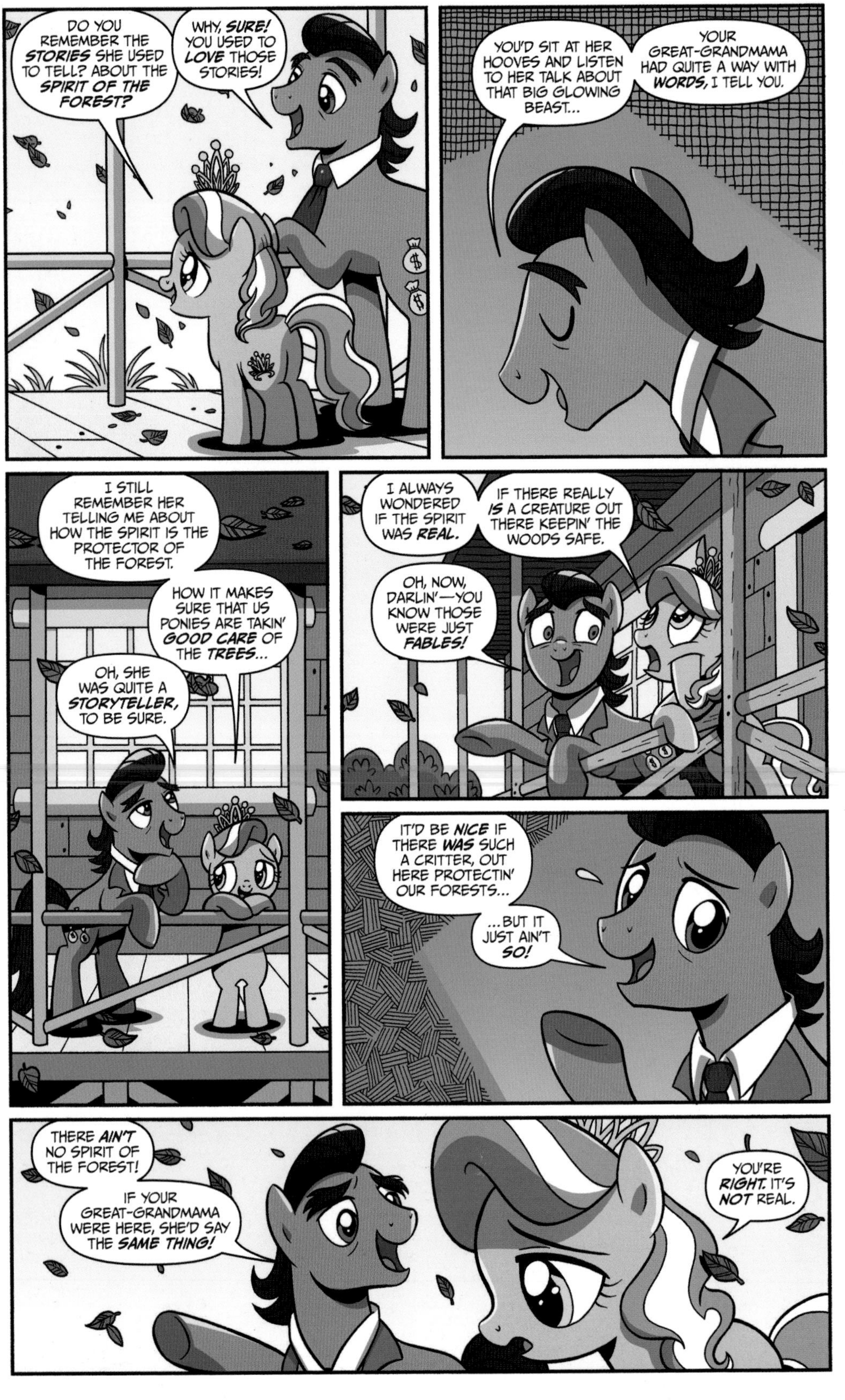
DO YOU REMEMBER THE *STORIES* SHE USED TO TELL? ABOUT THE *SPIRIT OF THE FOREST?*
WHY, *SURE!* YOU USED TO *LOVE* THOSE STORIES!
YOUR GREAT-GRANDMAMA HAD QUITE A WAY WITH *WORDS,* I TELL YOU.
YOU'D SIT AT HER HOOVES AND LISTEN TO HER TALK ABOUT THAT BIG GLOWING BEAST...
I STILL REMEMBER HER TELLING ME ABOUT HOW THE SPIRIT IS THE PROTECTOR OF THE FOREST.
HOW IT MAKES SURE THAT US PONIES ARE TAKIN' *GOOD CARE* OF THE *TREES*...
OH, SHE WAS QUITE A *STORYTELLER,* TO BE SURE.
I ALWAYS WONDERED IF THE SPIRIT WAS *REAL.*
IF THERE REALLY *IS* A CREATURE OUT THERE KEEPIN' THE WOODS SAFE.
OH, NOW, DARLIN'—YOU KNOW THOSE WERE JUST *FABLES!*
IT'D BE *NICE* IF THERE *WAS* SUCH A CRITTER, OUT HERE PROTECTIN' OUR FORESTS...
...BUT IT JUST AIN'T *SO!*
THERE *AIN'T* NO SPIRIT OF THE FOREST!
IF YOUR GREAT-GRANDMAMA WERE HERE, SHE'D SAY THE *SAME THING!*
YOU'RE *RIGHT.* IT'S *NOT* REAL.

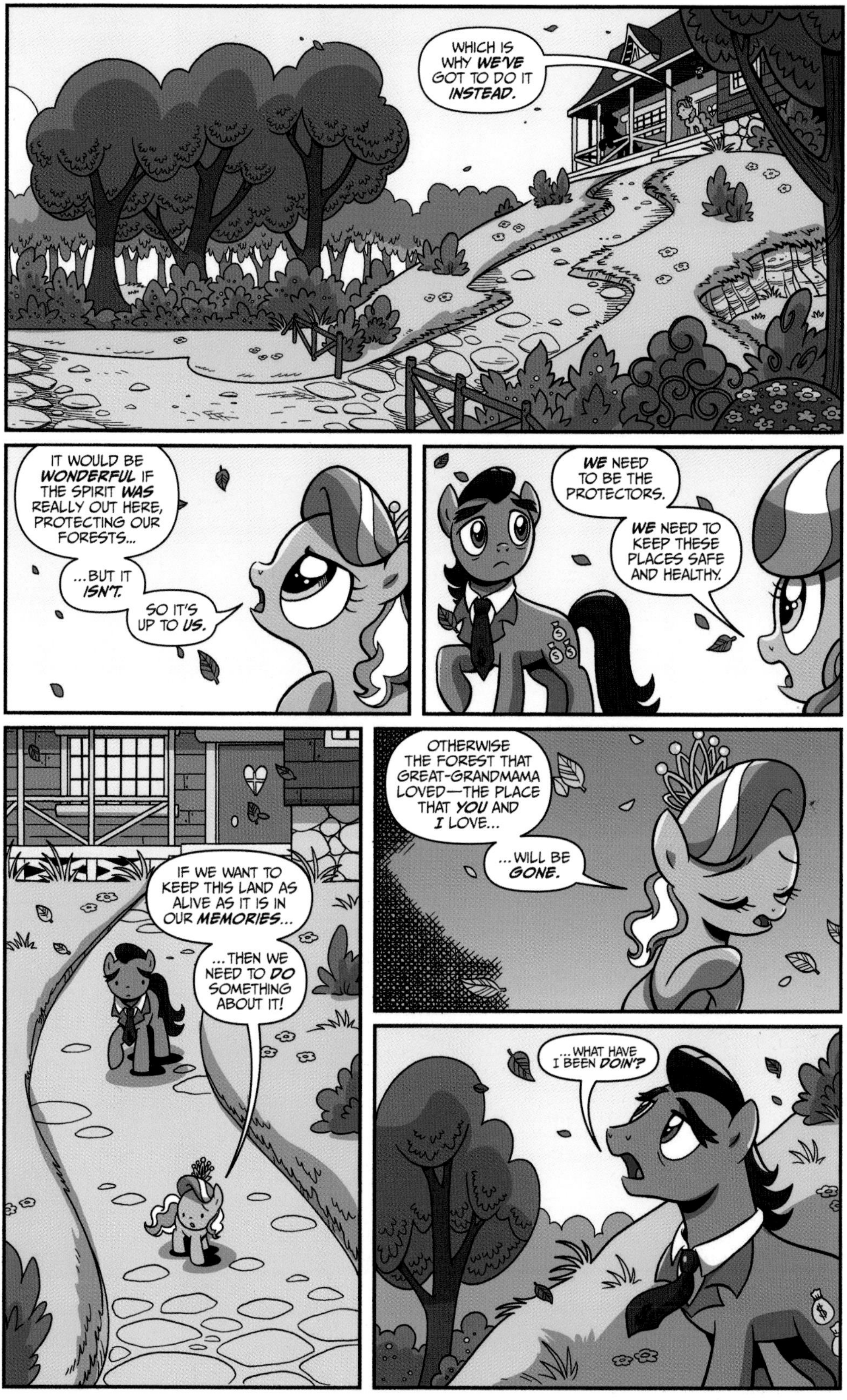
WHICH IS WHY WE'VE GOT TO DO IT INSTEAD.
IT WOULD BE WONDERFUL IF THE SPIRIT WAS REALLY OUT HERE, PROTECTING OUR FORESTS...
...BUT IT ISN'T.
SO IT'S UP TO US.
WE NEED TO BE THE PROTECTORS.
WE NEED TO KEEP THESE PLACES SAFE AND HEALTHY.
IF WE WANT TO KEEP THIS LAND AS ALIVE AS IT IS IN OUR MEMORIES...
...THEN WE NEED TO DO SOMETHING ABOUT IT!
OTHERWISE THE FOREST THAT GREAT-GRANDMAMA LOVED—THE PLACE THAT YOU AND I LOVE...
...WILL BE GONE.
...WHAT HAVE I BEEN DOIN'?

YOU'RE **ABSOLUTELY RIGHT!**

THESE WOODS ARE **SPECIAL** TO THIS FAMILY! AN' I'M GOING TO MAKE SURE THEY **STAY** SPECIAL!

TOMORROW, I'M GOING TO PUT IN AN ORDER:

NO LOGGING WITHIN **FIFTY FEET** OF GREAT-GRANDMAMA'S CABIN!

DAD...

YOU'RE **RIGHT!** A **HUNDRED** FEET!

NO, DAD, THAT'S **NOT** ENOUGH.

DON'T YOU **SEE?**

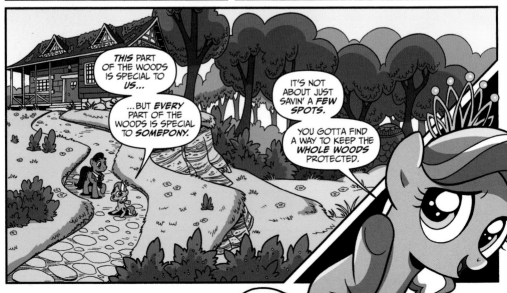

THIS PART OF THE WOODS IS SPECIAL TO **US**...

...BUT **EVERY** PART OF THE WOODS IS SPECIAL TO **SOMEPONY.**

IT'S NOT ABOUT JUST SAVIN' A **FEW** SPOTS.

YOU GOTTA FIND A WAY TO KEEP THE **WHOLE WOODS** PROTECTED.

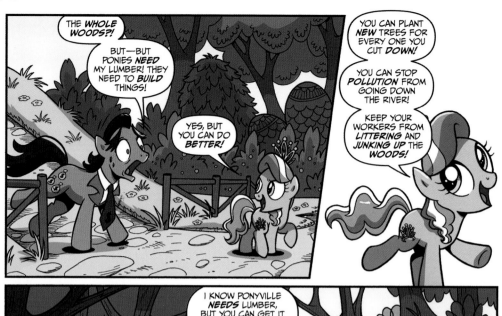

THE **WHOLE WOODS?!**

BUT—BUT PONIES **NEED** MY LUMBER! THEY NEED TO **BUILD** THINGS!

YES, BUT YOU CAN DO **BETTER!**

YOU CAN PLANT **NEW** TREES FOR EVERY ONE YOU CUT **DOWN!**

YOU CAN STOP **POLLUTION** FROM GOING DOWN THE RIVER!

KEEP YOUR WORKERS FROM **LITTERING** AND **JUNKING UP** THE **WOODS!**

I KNOW PONYVILLE **NEEDS** LUMBER, BUT YOU CAN GET IT WITHOUT **DESTROYING** THE WOODS!

MAYBE YOU WON'T MAKE AS MUCH **MONEY**—BUT THESE WOODS ARE **MORE IMPORTANT** THAN MONEY!

"MORE IMPORTANT THAN MONEY"...

I NEVER THOUGHT I'D **HEAR** THOSE WORDS.

AND I **CERTAINLY** NEVER THOUGHT I'D **AGREE** WITH THEM.

...YOU'RE **RIGHT**, MY LITTLE **DUMPLIN'**.

THERE'S GOT TO BE SOME **CHANGES** IN THE WAY I DO **BUSINESS!**

SO LET'S GET **STARTED!**

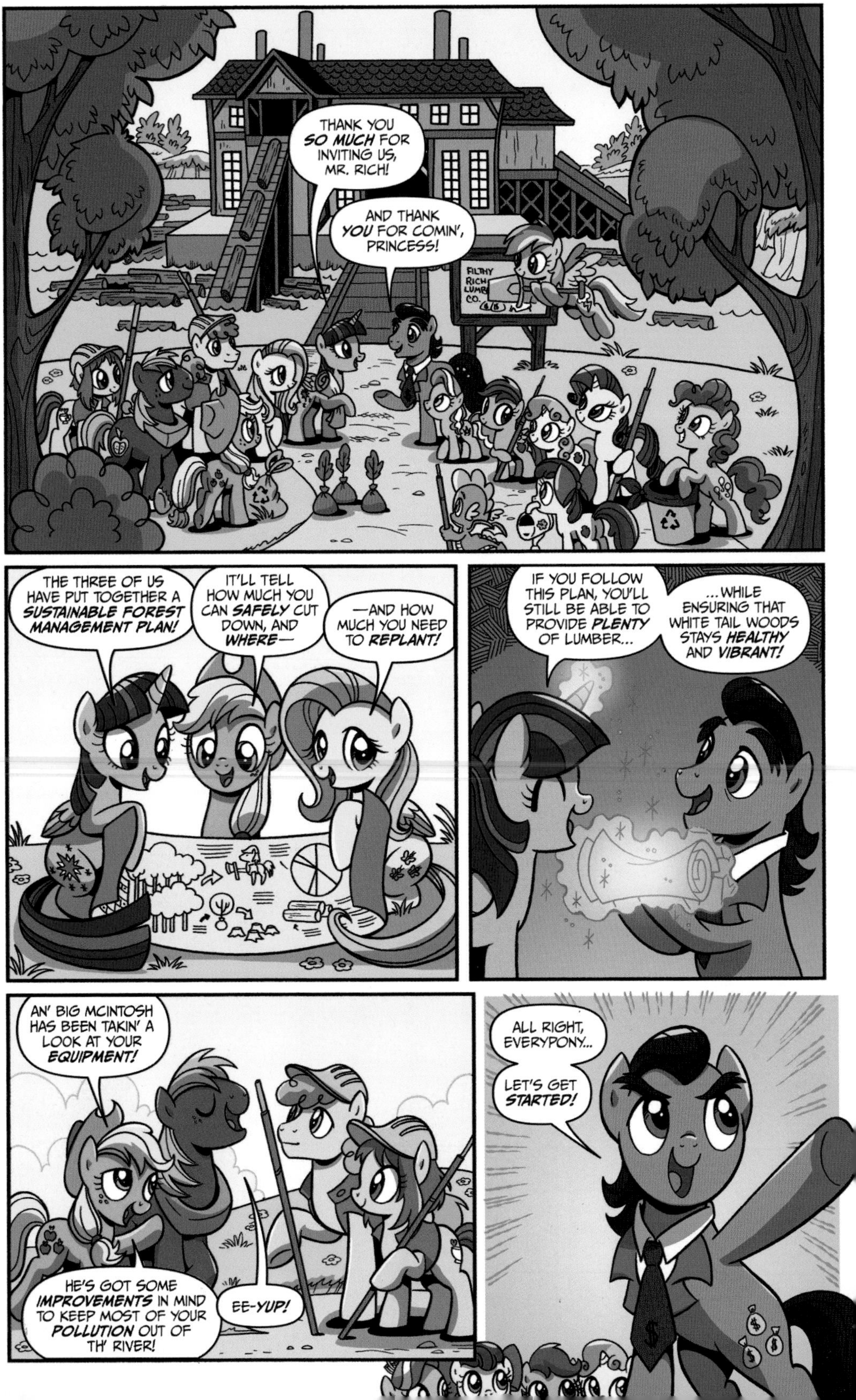
THANK YOU *SO MUCH* FOR INVITING US, MR. RICH!
AND THANK *YOU* FOR COMIN', PRINCESS!
FILTHY RICH
THE THREE OF US HAVE PUT TOGETHER A ***SUSTAINABLE FOREST MANAGEMENT PLAN!***
IT'LL TELL HOW MUCH YOU CAN *SAFELY* CUT DOWN, AND *WHERE*—
—AND HOW MUCH YOU NEED TO *REPLANT!*
IF YOU FOLLOW THIS PLAN, YOU'LL STILL BE ABLE TO PROVIDE *PLENTY* OF LUMBER...
...WHILE ENSURING THAT WHITE TAIL WOODS STAYS *HEALTHY* AND *VIBRANT!*
AN' BIG MCINTOSH HAS BEEN TAKIN' A LOOK AT YOUR ***EQUIPMENT!***
HE'S GOT SOME ***IMPROVEMENTS*** IN MIND TO KEEP MOST OF YOUR ***POLLUTION*** OUT OF TH' RIVER!
EE-*YUP!*
ALL RIGHT, EVERYPONY...
LET'S GET *STARTED!*

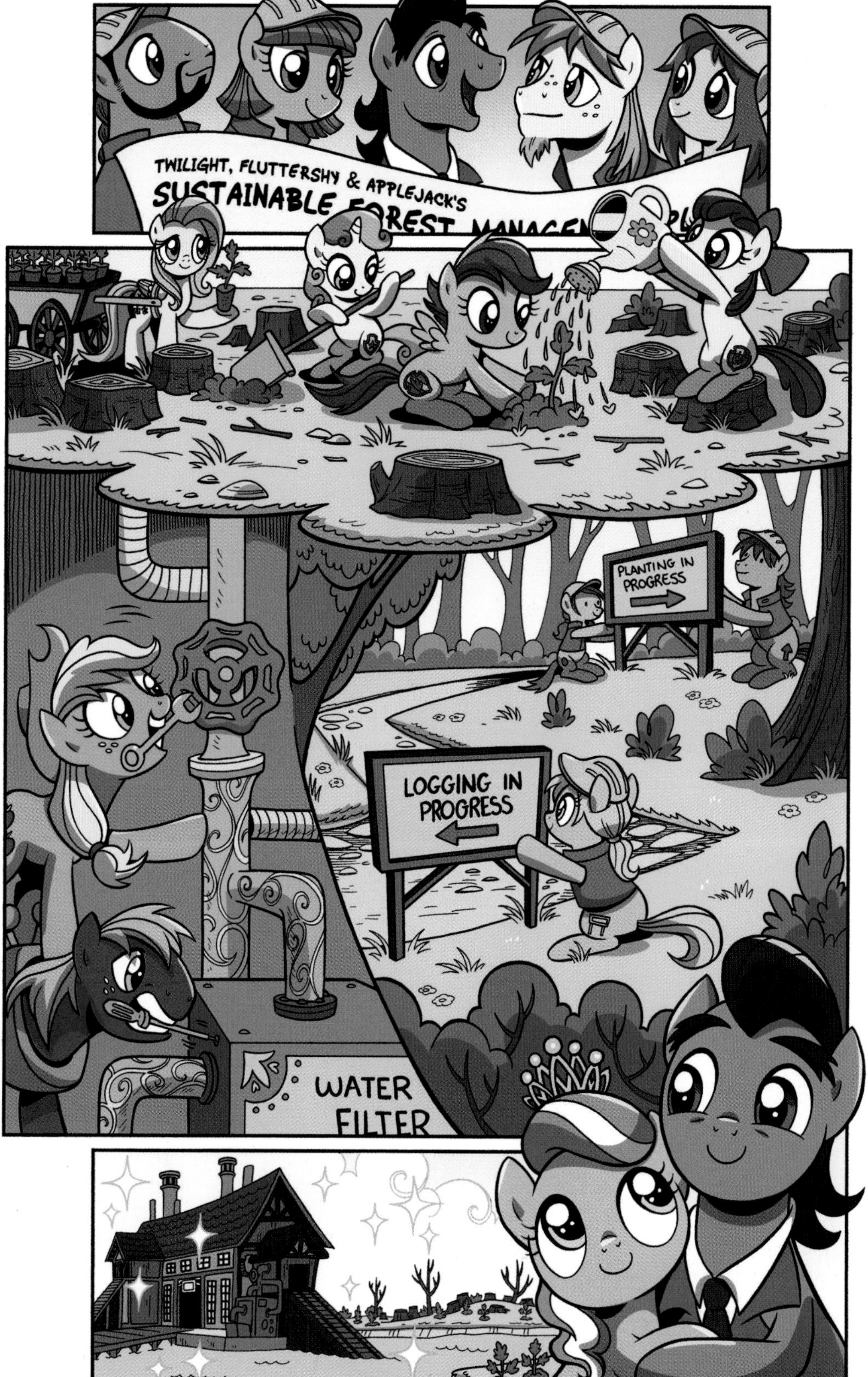
TWILIGHT, FLUTTERSHY & APPLEJACK'S
SUSTAINABLE FOREST MANAGEM
PLANTING IN PROGRESS
LOGGING IN PROGRESS
WATER FILTER

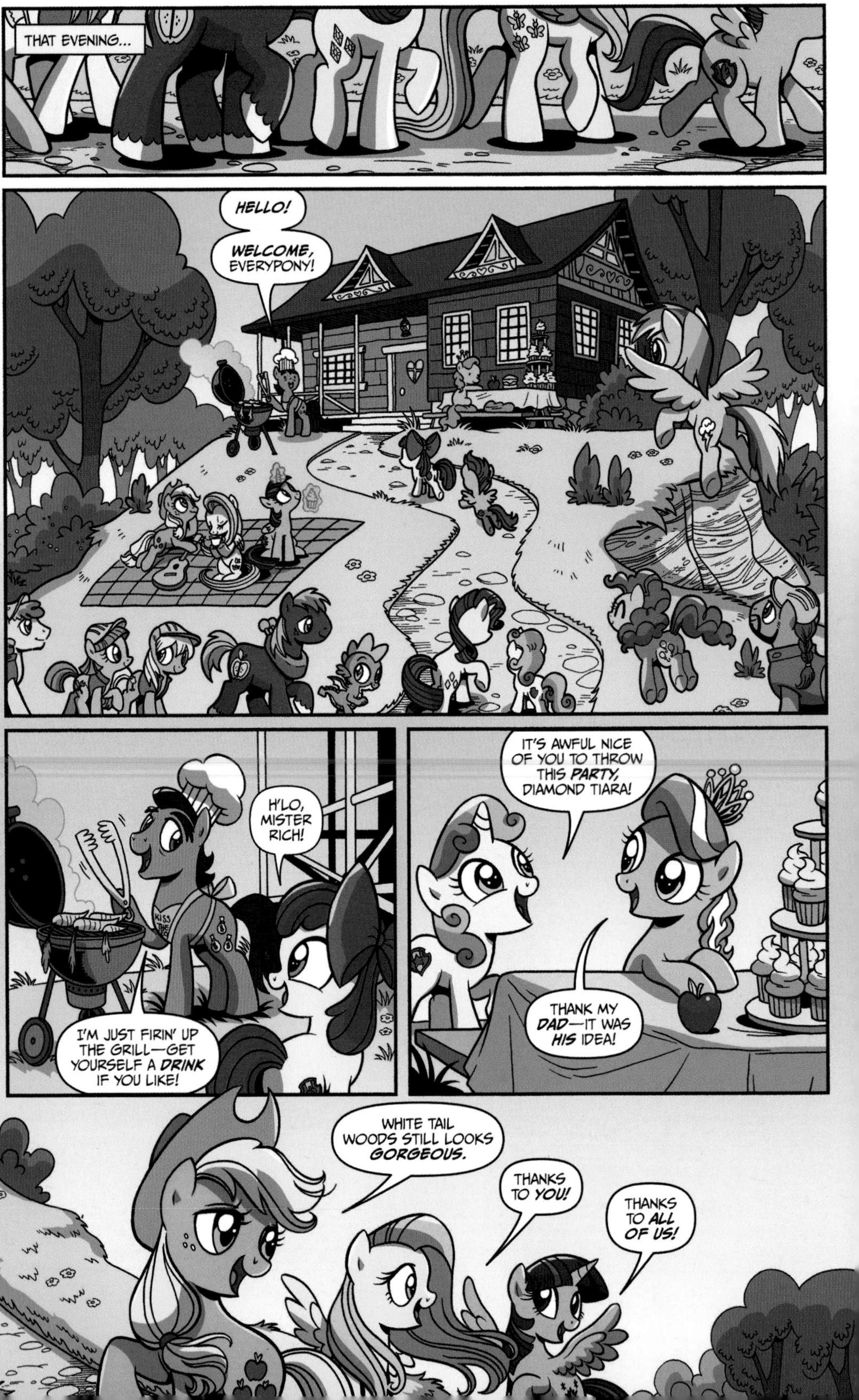
THAT EVENING...
HELLO!
WELCOME, EVERYPONY!
H'LO, MISTER RICH!
I'M JUST FIRIN' UP THE GRILL—GET YOURSELF A DRINK IF YOU LIKE!
IT'S AWFUL NICE OF YOU TO THROW THIS PARTY, DIAMOND TIARA!
THANK MY DAD—IT WAS HIS IDEA!
WHITE TAIL WOODS STILL LOOKS GORGEOUS.
THANKS TO YOU!
THANKS TO ALL OF US!

FRIENDS, **THANK YOU** FOR GATHERING HERE TONIGHT.

EVERY ONE OF YOU HAS HELPED ME BECOME A BETTER PONY...

...AND FIND A **BETTER WAY** OF DOIN' BUSINESS.

I WAS ABOUT TO **DESTROY** THESE BEAUTIFUL WOODS...

...ALL FOR A **FEW LOUSY BITS.**

I WOULD'VE **BETRAYED** THE MEMORY OF MY **GRANDMAMA** AND RUINED A PLACE FULL OF **HAPPY MEMORIES!**

IT TOOK **THESE BRAVE FILLIES**—

—AND **ESPECIALLY MY DAUGHTER**—

—TO SHOW ME TH' **ERROR** OF MY WAYS.

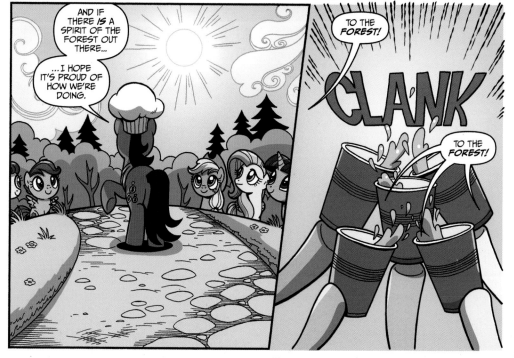

AND IF THERE **IS** A SPIRIT OF THE FOREST OUT THERE...

...I HOPE IT'S PROUD OF HOW WE'RE DOING.

TO THE **FOREST!**

CLANK

TO THE **FOREST!**

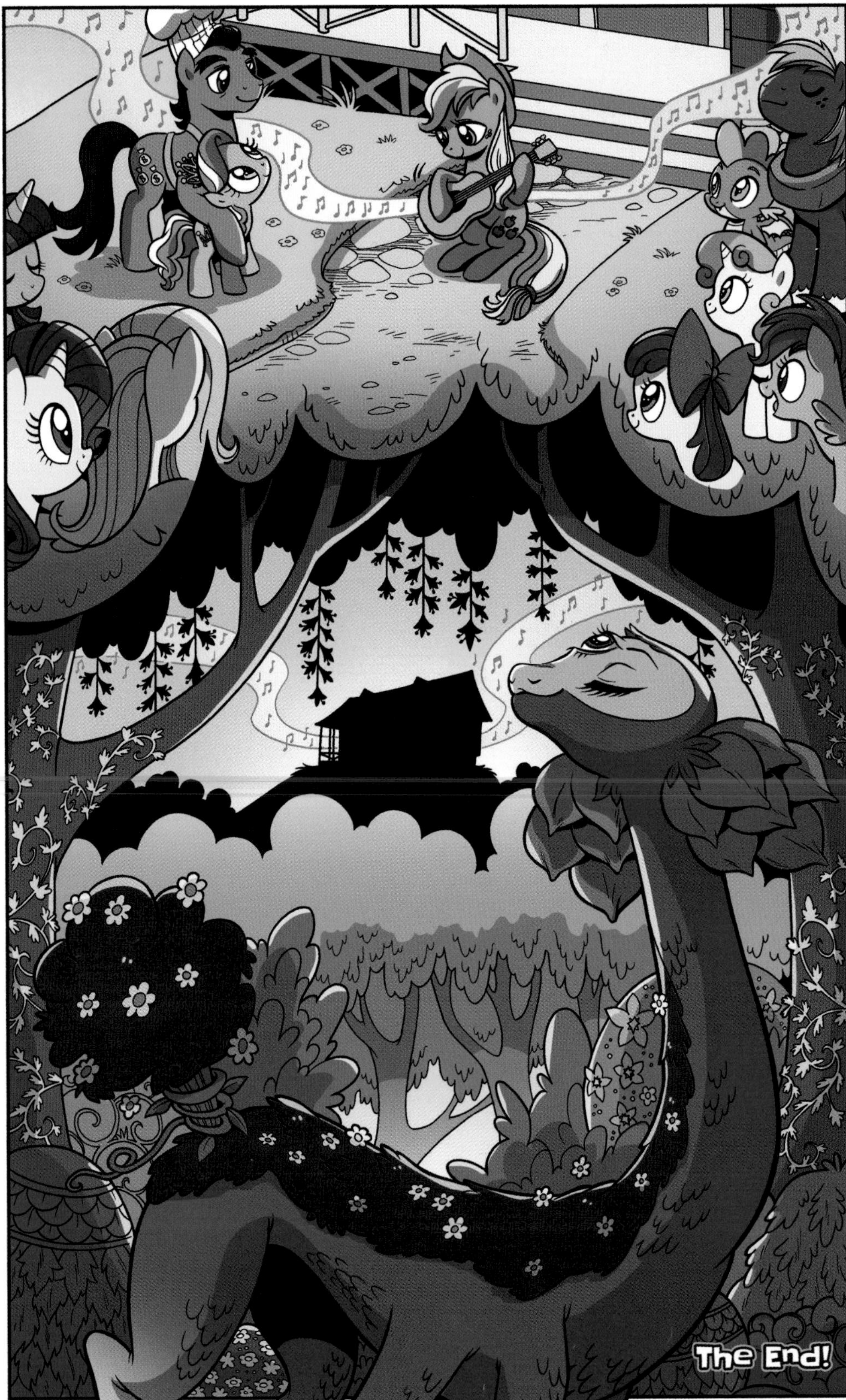
The End!

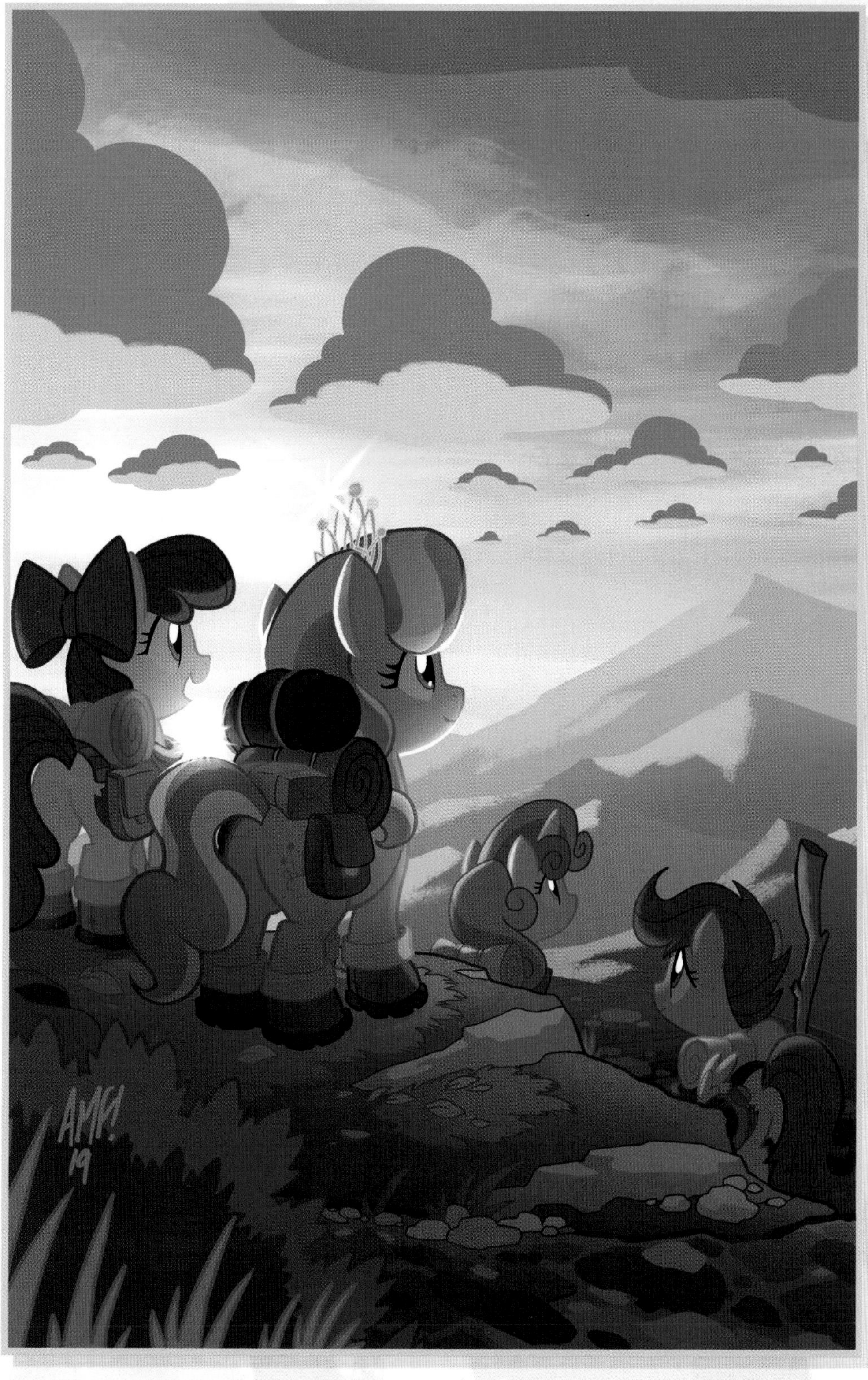
AMP!
19

ART BY **Tony Fleecs**

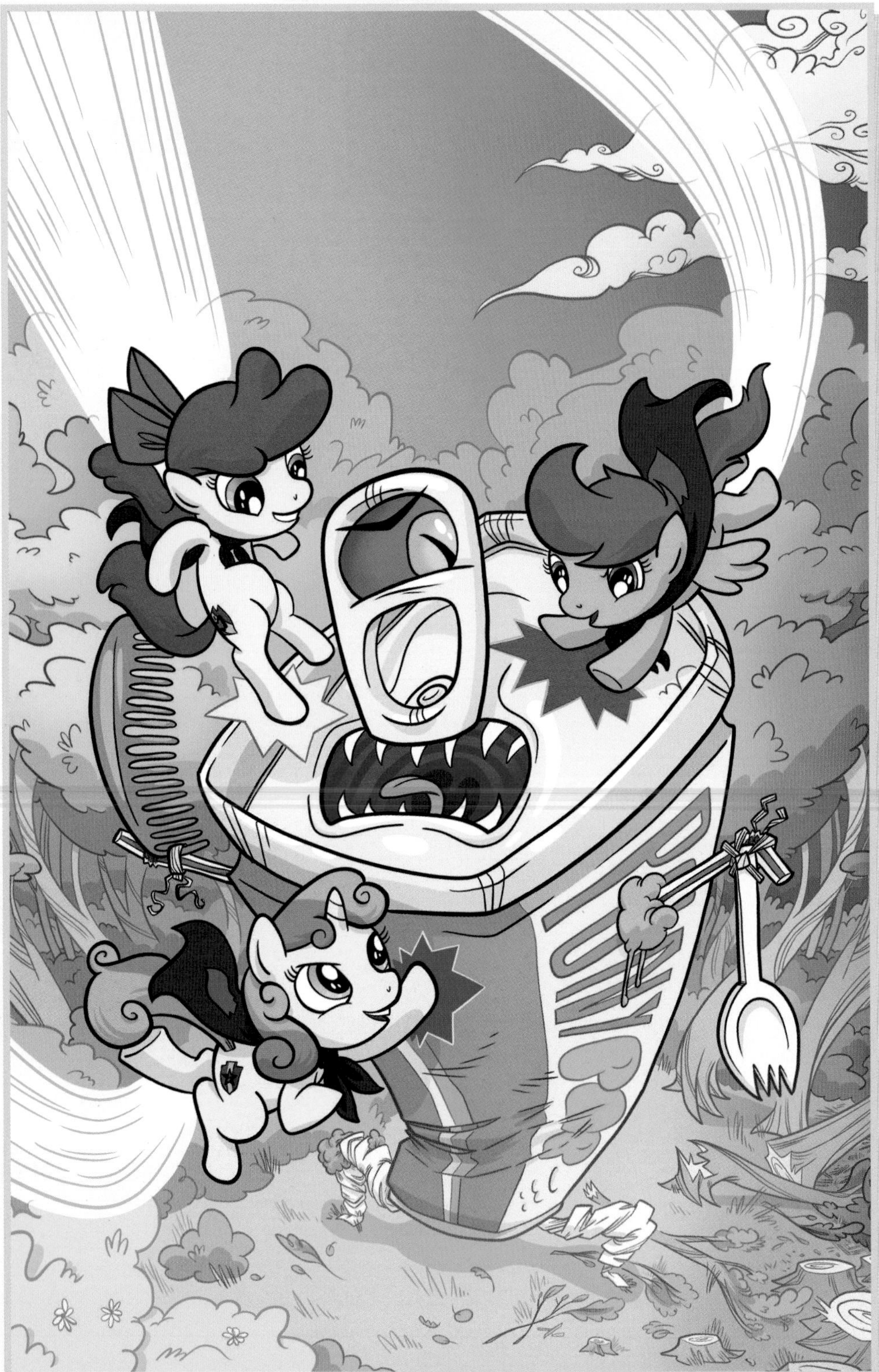

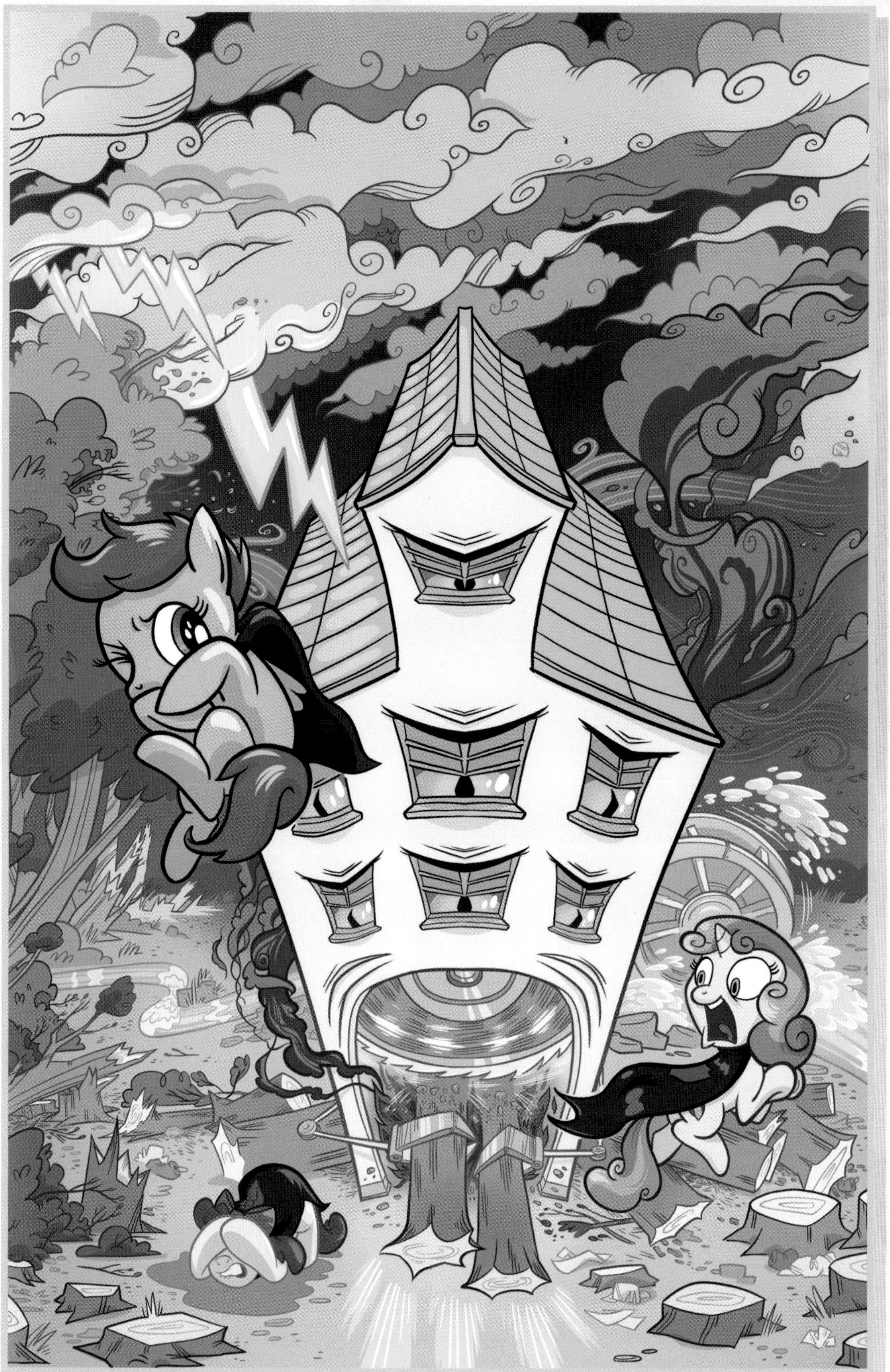

ART BY **Kate Sherron**

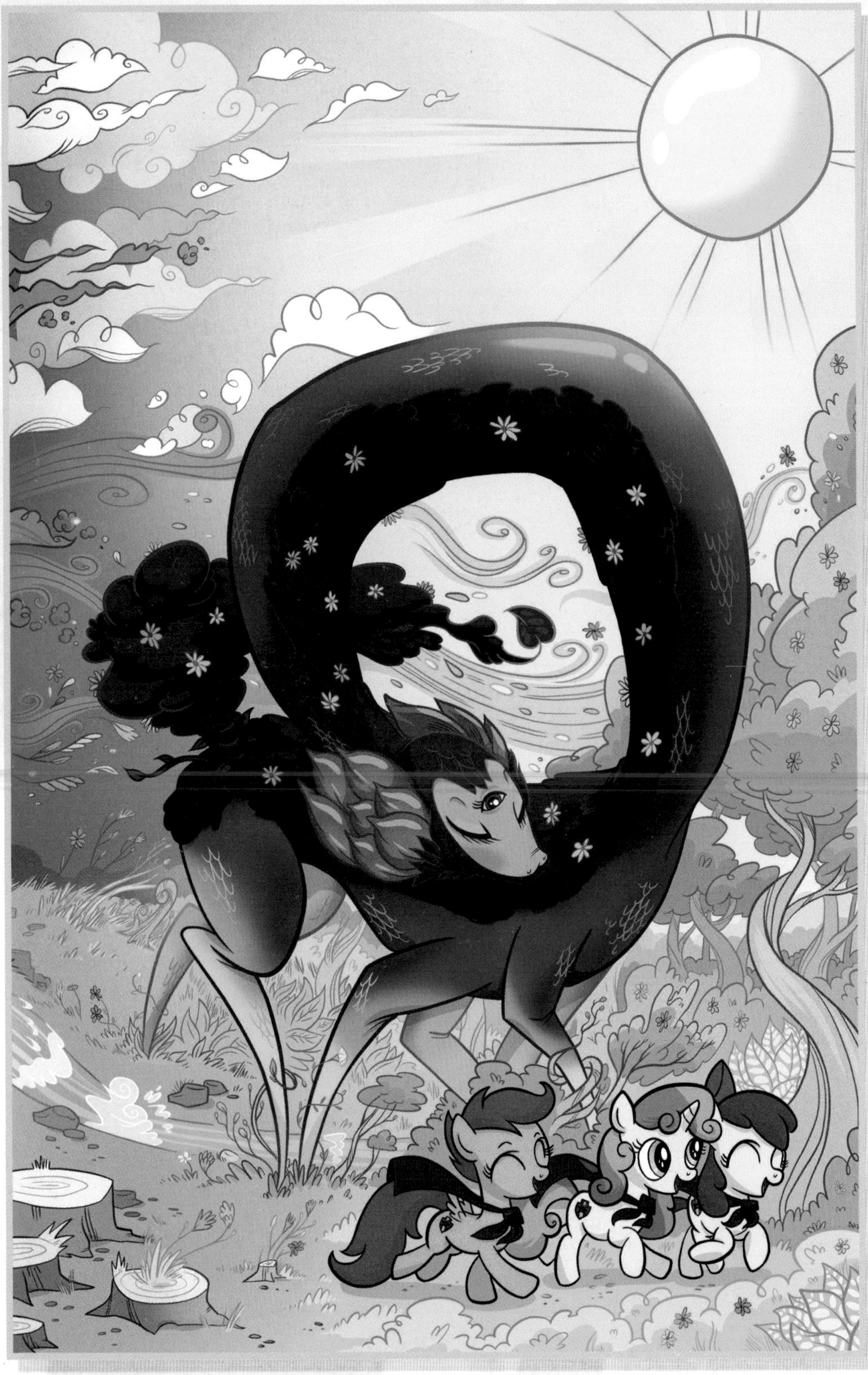

ART BY **Kate Sherron**